Half Truths Under a Broken Moon

by

Jody Wenner

Half Truths Under a Broken Moon

Cover Art by *The Wild Rose Press, Inc.*

The Wild Rose Press, Inc.
PO Box 708
Adams Basin, NY 14410-0708
Visit us at www.thewildrosepress.com

Publishing History
First Edition, 2023
Trade Paperback ISBN 978-1-5092-5227-5
Digital ISBN 978-1-5092-5228-2

Published in the United States of America

We turned the page of the album, ready to move on from that topic, and there was a small picture of me and Sonny sitting on a couch holding hands. It wasn't the plaid farm couch, so it had to have been in our apartment in Minneapolis. I'd probably looked at that picture a million times before, but now that I was older so many details stuck out to me that I hadn't seen before. The two of us didn't look at all like twins, even fraternal. Sonny had dark hair, dark eyes, and an olive complexion. I had lighter and paler features, blonde hair, and light green eyes. It was so strange that my mom named her for the sun and me for the moon, when it would have made more sense if they were switched based on our features.

But it was in the eyes, now that I was really examining the photo that I realized where I'd seen them before.

"Does Sonny look like anyone familiar to you?" I asked Brad, pointing at the picture of my sister.

"I was just thinking how she doesn't look like you at all," he said. "But familiar? I don't..."

"Your Uncle Mickey, maybe?"

Chapter One

At the end of the day, I found myself in a rental car in the parking lot of The Pigsty trying to decide if I honestly wanted to go in or not. I rolled down the window to get a little air. It was dusk. The stars were just starting to pop overhead. I hadn't seen the sky twinkle for a long time.

My hand reached for the keys dangling from the ignition. I could give one quick twist—and forget I'd ever contemplated this whole wacky idea in the first place. On the other hand, I'd had a miserable day and could really use a drink. Plus, this happened to be the only bar in the whole damn town.

I began nervously playing with the car keys while chewing on my own insecurities, remembering how enamored I'd been with this place as a kid. Back in the day, this lot was often packed with shiny Indians and Harleys. Passing by it appeared exciting and dangerous, unlike my own life on the farm. Alas, it was no longer a biker bar. It was now just your average small-town bar and grill. Yet, for some reason, it still held mystery and intrigue.

So, what was I waiting for? Here was my chance. Finally, after all this time, I was of age and able to go inside to see what all the fuss was about, and I was stalling. I'd been to a million dive bars before, but this one was different. This one was in my hometown. The place I'd purposely stayed away from for nearly a decade.

The parking lot wasn't filled with motorcycles anymore. In fact, it wasn't crowded at all. It wasn't that surprising given it was a weeknight well past the dinner rush. As my hand continued to fiddle with the car keys, I looked toward the stucco building. The sign over the entrance no longer blinked *The Pigsty* in neon yellow as it did when I was a kid. It was now a simple black sign with red paint that read *Finley and Sons*. Another reason why I was being indecisive.

I checked my face in the rearview mirror of the rental car. I looked like absolute hell, but under the circumstances, this was as good as it was going to get. I messed with my hair a bit, but to no avail. As the saying went, there was no point putting lipstick on a pig. Ironically, this place wasn't a pigsty any longer and it wasn't my home anymore either, so what did I care?

As the darkness washed over the parking lot, a single overhead street light activated. The stars were unaffected by the lone, dingy bulb, but I was clearly running out of time. If I put it off much longer, the decision would be made for me. It was now or never, so I took a deep breath as if it was the last bit of fresh air I would get, rolled up the window, yanked the keys from the ignition, and got out of the car.

The bell jingled when I walked in causing the bartender to turn his head toward me without really looking and give a quick wave. It was too dark in the place for him to have recognized me from this far away, even if he had been paying attention. As soon as I saw him, the dull throb in my temple sharpened a bit. I considered turning around, but I'd probably draw more attention to myself by doing so. Besides, I was going to see him eventually. This town was smaller than a Manhattan studio apartment. There was zero chance of me not running into him at some point while I was back. Why not just pull the bandage off now?

I sat down at the end of the bar, opposite where he stood near the taps washing out pint glasses. He chatted with a pretty server who hung over the edge of the bar leaning into him in a flirty way, which didn't surprise me in the least. Seeing him again brought more feelings to the surface than I expected, or at least different ones than I anticipated.

As my eyes started to adjust to the din, I tapped my anxiety out through my fingers onto the bar and looked around a bit while I waited to be served. As I'd surmised from the parking lot, the place was nearly empty. There were four people in a booth along the wall, and a few stools over from where I sat, an old couple clutched bottles of cheap beer, silently looking toward the back of the bar which had a shelf running the length of the wall lined with old pictures and dusty tchotchkes.

So, this was the forbidden place I'd imagined in my mind as being glamourous and exhilarating growing up. If only I'd have known back then that it was actually just a small, dank room with some tables and an old billiards table bolted to the floor near the bathroom. I imagine back in the day there was a jukebox playing cool tunes and thick cigarette smoke wafting through the small space, but tonight it was quiet, and the air was more musty than smoky. I understood the need for the low lighting. So much for being cheered up.

From my stool, I noted a few framed photos on the shelf directly in front of me. One in particular grabbed my attention. It was hard to make out all of the details from where I sat, but I was pretty sure it was Bob "Old Man" Finley and his three sons. The picture was obviously one from well before they purchased the biker bar and turned into a neighborhood joint. That happened at some point after I left. Bob wasn't even alive anymore.

They all looked fresh-faced and relatively happy in the picture. I could just make out Max wedged between his two brothers. I recognized his older brother Kenny on his left. They were both tall and lean, like their dad. Max wore a cowboy hat even at that age apparently. On the other end stood what I assumed was the middle brother. I didn't know his name or recall if I'd ever met him. He was a bit stockier than the rest of them. He had long, dark hair and a full beard and mustache covering his face. A red bandana wrapped around his forehead. He wore a leather motorcycle jacket with a cigarette dangled from his mouth. It seemed to me he would have fit in perfectly when the place was a biker bar.

I looked up as the bartender set a cardboard coaster down in front of me.

"What can I get for ya?" he asked. More clean-cut looking than the guys in the picture, there was still no question that he was a younger version of the tall and lean Finley sons, or one of them anyway. The sign should have read Finley and Sons and Sons.

"Um, I'll have a Hart's," I said just as he raised his gaze to meet mine for the first time.

"Luna?"

I smiled. "Brad Finley. You remembered me."

"Wow! You're the last person I was expecting to see." His return smile made me relax a bit. I suddenly felt like a teenager all over again. His dimples weren't as deep as they'd been when he was a pudgy-faced kid, but his hair was still brown and shaggy. His eyes were still playful and sensitive at the same time. Overall, he looked the same if a decade older, and it was comforting in a way I hadn't expected. "This is crazy! What are you doing here?"

"Grammy's sick," I said.

"God. That's right. I heard. I'm so sorry." He gently set his hand down on mine. My immediate response was to pull my own hand away, but I couldn't because I was instead doing everything I could not to show that my entire body was suddenly so warm I could hardly breathe.

"Let me grab you that beer," he said, relinquishing his hand from mine.

I breathed and nodded. "Thanks."

He set the can down along with an empty pint glass. I took a sip straight from the can and said, "You actually gave me my first Hart's. Do you remember that? I think we were maybe fifteen or sixteen at the time."

"I remember. On the hill, right?"

"Yeah."

"God. That feels like a lifetime ago," he said.

"And yet, nothing has changed, apparently," I said, examining the can which still had the same design on it.

He laughed. "True. Do you remember that time when we got the wild idea to camp out overnight on the hill? We begged and begged, and they finally let us. So, we took sleeping bags up there and got all set up and after like an hour, you were covered in mosquito bites, and I thought you were having some kind of allergic reaction."

I nodded. "I remember. I told you that I was probably allergic to you."

"We went back to the house and Gus made me sleep in the den," he said.

"I had forgotten that part, but it does not surprise me at all."

"Your grandpa still doesn't like me."

"GG doesn't like anybody," I said.

"True. So, how's New York?" he asked.

"It's nothing like here, so…I love it."

Shaking his head, Brad said, "I can't even imagine what it must be like to live in a big city like that."

"And I can't imagine what it must be like to have never left Alton, so…"

"Ouch," Brad said, covering his chest as if wounded.

"Sorry. I've always been too straightforward for this passive-aggressive Midwestern town. That's why they kicked me out, don't ya know?"

"They kicked you out, huh? This is the first time I'm hearing about it."

"It's true. This town has a secret code. The main one being: don't talk bad about Alton. They came for me in the night. I had no choice but to leave."

He smirked. "Really? Wow. I had no idea."

"It's a very guarded secret code. You wouldn't understand because you're one of the good ones. A loyal Altonian."

Brad nodded. "I guess that also explains why you've stayed away so long too," he said.

"Yes, well, I had no choice in the matter."

His tone changed from playful to serious. "You really didn't miss anything about this place?"

"I mean, sure. I missed my grandparents, and the river, but…"

"But not me?"

The question came out of left field and plunged directly into my heart. I didn't know how to answer it. I could barely look up at him, but when I did, I saw the hurt in his brown eyes that he quickly replaced with his signature deep-dimpled smile. "Well, I missed you," he said. His tone was warm and sincere and the essence of whom I had remembered him to be. If only I could have been as forthcoming with my own emotions.

"I…" I wanted to explain to him that it wasn't about him. That he was the only reason I might have actually stayed. That he was my best friend and I thought about him all the time, which did not explain at all why I hadn't stayed in touch, but instead, I said, "You know why I had to go."

The door jingled and he looked over at the customers entering—a group of middle-aged men in matching shirts that said Alton Rec Softball—before turning back to me. "I gotta take care of this, but I'll check back with you as soon as I can," he said, heading toward the row of taps on the other end of the bar.

Sitting with my can of beer, I watched Brad out of the corner of my sightline pouring drinks while the cute, perky server leaned into him once again. He said something to her, and she laughed, bouncing her shoulders while swinging her long hair back. I wondered if they were dating. I knew he wasn't married because I may have casually asked my grandpa earlier that day, but to think Brad Finley would be nearing thirty and single would have been foolish. I still couldn't believe he asked if I'd missed him. What kind of question was that? I was here now, wasn't I? That had to tell him something.

When he returned, he said, "Can I get you another?"

"No. It's almost as bad as I remember it," I said,

pushing the can of cheap beer toward him.

He laughed.

"Got anything a little stronger?" I asked.

He raised his brow at me. "Rough day?"

"Well, let's see, I just spent the last four hours trapped with my mother in a hospital room the size of a postage stamp with my dying grandma lying in the bed between us, so you be the judge."

He nodded. "What's your pleasure?"

"Whiskey coke?"

"Coming right up."

When he set my drink down, I said, "Thanks. Hey...how's your dad doing?"

"He's doing well. I suspect you'll see him at the farm at some point."

"I hope so. I've missed Max. Oh," I said, pointing to the picture on the wall. "Who's the guy on the far right, next to him in that old photo?"

Brad swiveled around. He plunked the picture from the shelf and handed it to me. "Him?" He pointed to the man with the red bandana and beard.

"Yeah."

"That's my uncle Mickey."

"Why have I never seen him before?"

"Uncle Mickey's a lot like you."

"Huh?"

"He didn't follow the first rule of Alton. He got on his bike one night, and under the cover of darkness, he hightailed it away from here...never to be seen again."

"Seriously?"

"Yep." Brad's tone continued with a mocking ghost story vibe. "Some say he was the black sheep and couldn't live up to my grandfather's expectations, while others say he did something so bad, there was no coming back from it." Brad chuckled. "I'm guessing it was much simpler than all the rumors. I think he just hated it here. Like you. But the legend of Uncle Mickey remains a mystery. Nobody really knows why he left for sure."

"Wow. Sounds like he may have broken a few more rules than I did."

"Yeah. He was a real rebel. I mean, just look at the guy," Brad said.

And that's exactly what I was doing. Now that the photo was right in front of my eyes, I could see it more clearly. Too clearly, in fact. Because maybe Brad wasn't all that far from the truth. There was something about Mickey, something eerily familiar. I wasn't exactly sure what it was about him until I homed in on his eyes. I knew those dark eyes. I hadn't seen them in over twenty years, but I would never forget them. They were the eyes of my twin sister.

I sucked in stale air and beer, and as I did, my vision suddenly went blurry. The slight headache I'd had when I walked in went full bore and my chest constricted at the exact moment my heart began to race. Shit! It was happening again.

"Sorry. I-I have to go." I got up and started to dig into my bag in search of my wallet, but it was difficult given that my vision was pinched and the room was spinning.

"Luna? Hey, are you okay?" Brad asked.

"Yeah. I'm just...not feeling well suddenly."

"You don't owe me anything for the drinks," he said, waving off the money I started yanking out.

"Thanks. It was nice to see you," I said, as I headed toward the door.

"Are you sure you're okay?" he called. "I can take you home."

"No! I'm good. I'm sure I'll see you again before I leave."

"I hope so," he said, but his tone was replete with doubt. I couldn't say that I blamed him for being skeptical. I wasn't sure why I couldn't just tell him what was going on. I always thought by keeping this secret from him, I wouldn't look totally and utterly bananas, but I was starting to realize that it actually made me look even more nuts than if I had just been truthful with him in the first place. What was wrong with me? Well, that was obviously the million-dollar question.

Chapter Two

The next morning, I was back at the hospital sitting in the suffocatingly small room with my mother. I felt like I had a hangover even though I'd hardly had time to take a few sips of my drink before I made my embarrassing escape from the bar. The lingering effects were always the same. My chest was still tense and my head throbbed like someone was banging on a drum inside my skull.

It was the real reason why I fled this place ten years ago. I hadn't necessarily run from my horrible relationship with my mother even though that was what I told Brad at the time. And I hadn't run to get away from the lingering trauma the death of my twin sister held over me, as much as leaving did help ease the pain of it. I hadn't even fled to get away from the awkward and undefined feelings that Brad and I had for one another. The truth was, not more than twenty-four hours after returning to my hometown, the panic attacks that had plagued my childhood were back.

My mom shot quick looks at me but said nothing. She sat on one side of Grammy's hospital bed while I was positioned on the other. Grammy was in the final throes of breast cancer. The heavy pain medications running through her IV made her unaware of our presence at this point. Her breathing was jagged. The only real sign of life was the slow beeps from the monitors. She was withered and yellow. Her hair was gone. Holding her hand, it felt like I was caressing a skeleton. I could hardly look at her. She'd once been a sturdy and strong farm woman, and that was how I wanted to remember her.

The room was chilly, way too chilly even for a spring day in Minnesota. It was likely not due to the air pumping out the vent immediately overhead. No. It was most certainly emanating from my mother. Her cold, rigid disposition cooled my bones in the exact way the drafty farmhouse windows made me shiver during a frigid Minnesota winter when I was younger.

But I was now rounding on thirty; I couldn't let her icy walls prevent me from asking the question I needed to ask. I tugged my cardigan around me like it was a shield, and said, "Mom, I want to find my dad."

She didn't even glance up at me this time. Her eyes continued to bore down onto Grammy as the words raced from her mouth without a moment of consideration, "Absolutely not."

"That's the thing. It's not a question. I'm an adult. I have a right to know who my father is."

Her tone remained even as she switched her gaze out the small hospital window. "This isn't really the time, Luna. If you've forgotten, we're here for your grandmother."

My voice, on the other hand, rose like an opera singer. "It's never the right time though, is it? I'm not sure why you're so scared to tell me. I highly doubt the earth is going to open up and suck you into it if you divulge who my father is." I paused, trying to steady myself. "Does it have anything to do with Sonny dying? Are you afraid to tell him about what happened to her?

Is that it? Because it's been such a long time, and I'm sure he'd probably want to know that one of his daughters is…" I couldn't form the words. Instead I said, "I think he'd want to know about us."

She finally looked at me. "Don't you think that if your father wanted to meet you, he'd have reached out by now? He's had twenty-seven years to do so."

"I…"

The snowball that my mother, the ice queen, released hit so hard and fast I wasn't able to dodge it. I was suddenly freezing and the light sweater I had on could do nothing to protect me against the harshness of it, so I got up and walked out of the room. It was my one defense. Ten years and nothing had changed. My mom and I still could not agree on a single thing and all I could do was run away when it got tense between us.

I bumped into Grandpa Gus who was pacing the hallway. "You should go in and sit down for a bit," I said to him, patting his shoulder. "Take a rest."

"I'll rest when I'm dead."

That was my GG. For all his talk of death though, he seemed to have hardly aged in the time I'd been gone, appearing more or less the same—rail thin, yet somehow strong as an ox for a man who was nearly eighty. He wore a pair of rust-brown coveralls with a white undershirt peeking out just over the top button. On his feet was the same pair of leather work boots he'd had for the past thirty years. The one slight difference in his appearance was that where there had once been thick, coffee brown facial hair that matched his head, there was now just a thin stubble of silver. I assumed his head matched his face in that regard, but he wore a brown stocking cap over it.

We parted ways as he continued to walk out his troubles. I, conversely, found the vending machines nestled in the middle of the hallway halfway between the ICU and the Labor and Delivery area. That felt about right to me. Somewhere in the middle of life and death was just…snacks. Nothing more, nothing less. I lingered in front of the machine for longer than necessary, giving myself some needed space from my mother, letting my anger fizzle. It was amazing how much less stifling the air felt out here. I breathed it in.

I eventually selected what I called a pop when I was a little girl in Minnesotan. As an adult New Yorker, I referred to it as a soda. I rarely drank the stuff anymore, but since this machine didn't dispense anything stronger, I was forced to compromise with liquid sugar. I got some candy to go with it for good measure.

I plopped down in a chair just outside of Grammy's room with my junk food. I was nowhere near ready to go back inside to quietly stew. I could do that all by myself. A part of me wished I could be more assertive, but what was I going to do? I doubted anything beyond strangling my mother until she revealed her secrets would work. I'd been trying to get answers from her since I was a teenager. She was a sealed vault.

And after talking to her just now, a part of me wondered if she was right. Why hadn't my father ever tried to contact me? I had grappled with this question before, but it was the first time someone else had said it directly to me. As a kid, on my lonelier days, I imagined him driving up to the farmhouse to whisk me away from there like he was a superhero, but the reality of it was that my father had never come around. Not once. I wasn't sure if it was because of something my mother had done or said, or if it was because of something she hadn't done or said. I had suspicions that she'd never told the man responsible for creating twin girls that we had even existed. That would explain her reluctance to share his name with me now. And yet, even after all these years, I was still hoping he might come to my rescue and save me. From what? Her? Myself? I wasn't sure. It was childish, but I couldn't let it go.

It wasn't that I didn't love being raised by GG and Grammy. They were both wonderful and nurturing people. If not for them, I couldn't imagine what my life would have been like. And I didn't want to blame my mom for being unable to care for me after Sonny died, but she became what GG referred to as troubled.

The thing that bothered me the most was that she gave up her rights to me. She dropped me with my grandparents at the age of four and she signed me away to them. I was legally theirs. I hardly knew them. And then she disappeared. At first, it was for long periods of time, only coming for short visits. Eventually, she was suddenly around more and more, but even when she stayed at the farm for stretches of time, she never seemed to give me the attention I craved. It wasn't until I was a teenager when she actually moved back in, when she began trying here and there to connect with me, but by then it was too late. I was angry with her for leaving me, and she was unwilling to explain anything to me about where she was, or what she'd been doing. She had no answers to the myriad of questions I had about what had happened to my twin sister and the mysterious circumstances that led to her death. In fact, we didn't talk about Sonny at all. All I was told was that it was a burglary and the only thing I remembered about it was the blood splattered all over the wall of our apartment the next day. Yet, something never added up about it, because we were living in a dumpy apartment in the cities. Mom was young, twenty-one years old, a college drop out. She was raising two toddlers and waiting tables. She was barely making rent. We had nothing. Why would someone want to rob us? And why kill a four year old in the process?

When I was about eight or nine, and in the third grade, my panic attacks started. They gradually got worse, to the point that I was scared to go anywhere because I wouldn't remember things afterward and come out of it in a fog. I was so worried about it happening at school, afraid I would be the laughing stock of my class, so Grammy started homeschooling me. The joke GG made was that I wasn't homeschooled, I was farm-schooled.

As I aged, I realized I was more like my mom than I wanted to admit. Troubled. And that made the two of us clash harder than ever. I blamed her for everything. So when I was seventeen, I took my high school exams by mail and I applied for colleges. I got as far away as I could. And the attacks stopped. But the desire to know who my father was never stopped. Something about seeing that photo at The Pigsty last night made it even stronger, and the fact that it triggered a panic attack at the same time made me think the two things were somehow connected. Since my mother wouldn't tell me anything, I wondered if Max might know something. He was Mickey's brother after all.

Chapter Three

Later that afternoon, Mom got up from her chair at Grammy's side, and said, "I should probably take Grandpa back to the house for some rest."

"I don't mind taking him," I said. I'd been staying at the hotel one town over next to the hospital and hadn't been back to the farm yet. I was anxious to see it, so this was my chance. Surprisingly, my mom didn't argue with me. It was the first thing we hadn't fought about since I'd stepped off the plane.

I wandered around the hospital for a while looking for GG. I found him sitting in the cafeteria clutching a glass of milk. His eyes were far away. My heart broke for him, but there was nothing I could do to fix it. I knew him. He wasn't one to talk much about things, especially his feelings. I understood and respected that. Grammy had always advised me to just, "leave him be." Having lived with him for all those years, I knew she was right. He was a loving man, but you couldn't push it. He showed affection differently, but he and I generally understood one another.

I sat down across from him. Gently, I said, "You wanna get out of here for a little while?"

He nodded, and we were off.

****

There was a certain comfort I found in driving through the winding hills of Alton, even as I took in the inevitable changes. This part of town, what they called the Upper Valley was farm country, but crops of new housing developments had popped up in spots that used to be, well, actual crops. It still felt lush with trees and rolling fields, especially in comparison to New York.

Although Alton was a small town, it wasn't completely uncomplicated. There were rich farmers on the top of the valley and a more working-class community in the heart of the lower valley near the main street along the riverfront. With that came some divisiveness in terms of the haves and have-nots, but overall it maintained a small town atmosphere for the most part.

GG didn't say much on the drive. He looked tired, so I let him rest while I wrestled with my emotions coasting down the familiar streets of my youth. The wooden signpost hung on a decorative piece of wrought iron sunk into the ground near the road read: *Andersen Farm Est. 1918* in faded black lettering. Below the name in much smaller letters it said: *Alton, MN.*

Turning into the property, I slowed down on the narrow gravel driveway as we approached the house. I had sudden flashes of Grammy standing on the front porch in her light-blue house dress, shaking out a rug, or shucking corn, or perpetually sweeping the steps. The thoughts threatened to unravel me, but I kept my emotions in check for GG's sake.

I parked the car off to the left side of the house, in front of the garage, and stepped out cautiously, taking in the scents. When the cool spring air—sweet, pungent, and familiar—hit my nose, the tension I held in my body went slack. I was home. I hadn't anticipated feeling so at ease with that. If anything, I thought the opposite would be true. So many memories, too many emotions attached.

The house, a pale yellow, spacious, three-story take on a classic turn-of-the-century farmhouse, was actually built in the 1950s after my grandparents got married and took over the land from GG's parents. The color had faded somewhat, and the paint on some of the siding was chipped and flaking. The rounded white columns on either side of the wrap-around porch still appeared sturdy if a little tired.

Instead of heading toward the house, GG got out of the rental car and went straight in the direction of the barn that sat directly behind and between the garage and house.

"Where are you going?" I asked him.

"To milk."

"Mom said you should rest."

"The cows say otherwise. Come on. Help me. It will be just like old times. You still remember how?"

"Of course I remember."

"Prove it," he challenged.

I pivoted away from the house and followed my grandfather. Passing the old porch swing on the far end, I couldn't believe it was still there, though it had seen better days. It tugged at my heart and I brushed my hand along the backside of it as I made my way around it on the path toward the cow barn.

Within a few minutes, GG was already bent low on his milking stool, a pipe dangling from his mouth, taking refuge from his emotions the way any old farmer would, I supposed. If only it were so easy for me.

"Grab your stool," he said to me. "It's in the same spot you left it."

I found the wooden three-legged milking stool

mounted on the nail about halfway up the wall. When I pulled it down, I turned it over, running my finger over the two letters etched into the wood by GG's hand at least two decades ago. Lu. It was the only name he'd ever called me, and I loved him for it. I never settled into my name. My mother said she named us Sonny and Luna because we were her Sun and Moon. I guess Luna was better than being named Moon. I only wish my mother's sentiment had held any water.

While he called me Lu, I was the only one who called him GG. Grandpa Gus was a mouthful and while Gram always called him Gussy, I wanted something all my own. She helped me come up with it when I first came to live with them, and it stuck.

Only two cows were tied to the milking posts. He never had a ton of them since this wasn't a cattle or dairy farm. The main crops were soy and corn. He just had an affinity for being self-sufficient and he enjoyed the big animals.

I set the stool down next to the brown heifer on GG's right and settled in. It took me a minute to find my rhythm again, but it came back.

"GG? Why did you decide to become a farmer?" This was a new question, one I'd never thought to ask him as a young girl. I had no idea why it had popped into my head, but it felt like a good distraction from everything else crowding the space up there.

"In my day," he said, "you didn't choose to become a farmer; if your daddy owned a farm, you were gonna be a farmer too. That was that. End of story."

"If your dad hadn't been a farmer, what do you think you would have done?"

He let out a puff of smoke. "I never thought about

20

it."

"Never?"

He shrugged. "I couldn't change it. Why dream?"

"That's sort of sad. But you like it, right? Being a farmer?"

"Got nothing to compare it to." He paused, like he always did when he needed to mull something over. "Course, I like the straightforwardness of it. You plant, you water, things grow, you harvest them. No gray areas. I don't like gray areas."

"No. Me neither."

We milked for a bit and then I said, "Where's Max? I thought he did most of the work around here now."

"He's probably around here somewhere. He does the bulk of it, but I still like to get my hands dirty occasionally."

"I saw Brad yesterday. I guess he's taken over at the bar."

GG snorted.

"What?"

"Nothing."

"You don't approve of him running the bar?"

"Not my place to approve or disapprove."

"You expected him to help Max here, didn't you?"

"I learned a long time ago to not expect much from people."

"Not everybody loves farming," I said.

"Max does."

"So you assumed his son would be like him."

"Brad was a good kid."

"Seems like he still is."

GG snorted again. "You should head inside and relax."

"You should, too."

"I got a couple more things to do here, and then I'll be in."

"Promise?"

"You sound just like yer Grammy."

"Somebody's gotta keep you in line," I teased.

"I'll be in soon. You get now and give this old man some peace."

Before going to the house, I circled the barn and headed to the orchard on the western edge of the property. It wasn't a huge orchard, just a dozen or so small apple trees, but they were special, or at least one of them was. I had so few memories of my twin sister and most were fuzzy at best, but this one was as clear as that crisp autumn day. We were three years old when Mom brought us to the farm for a visit. While the adults chatted on the porch, we were allowed to roam the property. Sonny was a bundle of energy, while I was pensive. She was always far more adventurous than me. She pulled me along, seeking out excitement. When we got to the apple trees, they were heavy with shiny red balls that were just beyond our reach.

Sonny immediately found a stick and began to bat at the smallest tree, jumping up and down with delight, attempting to get a juicy prize from the tree. I wasn't sure if it was a good idea, being reserved and scared. What I was scared about, I couldn't say now. Maybe it was the impending doom that was to befall my twin just a short time later. Maybe it was the crazed spirit she had as she swung the stick at the innocent fruit. To me, my sister was being reckless, out of control. I kept telling her to stop, that we should head back to the house, but she didn't listen to me.

Finally, she made contact and an apple fell from the limb. She whooped and cheered and grabbed it up. I had no idea what she would do with it, but she turned and handed it to me. I stood looking at it like I'd never seen an apple before.

"Eat it!" she said.

I was hesitant. Were we allowed? Was it safe? Would we get in trouble?

She swung her bat again and again as I pondered the apple in my hand. She finally managed to get another one to drop. She polished it off on her shirt and we sat down under the tree. I watched Sonny gobble up her apple. I remember the unbridled joy she had on her face as she did it. I did not eat mine. Instead, I carried it back to the house and gave it to my mother. I wasn't sure if it was to tattle on my sister, or if I was asking for approval to eat the apple. Either way, my mother took it from me, set it down on the porch rail dismissively, and continued to chat with Grammy and GG. And that was that.

After Sonny died, we spread her ashes under that exact tree, the one they called the runt of the pack. I found it now and stopped in front of it. My arms hugged my chest. She was still here, in this very dirt. My twin. My other half. I hadn't visited this spot on the property much growing up, after we put her ashes down. I don't know why. I just couldn't get myself to do it, but since moving, I'd thought of this little spot so much, it was practically imprinted into my brain. And I'd transferred it into drawings using ink, charcoal, and pastels. I'd painted it with watercolor, oils, and acrylics on sticky notes, sketch pads, printer paper, and canvases. I knew this spot inside and out. It had taken on a life of its own in the property of my head. But nothing compared to being here in person.

The trees were just starting to come back to life after what I could only expect was a long and brutally cold winter. Another perk of leaving this place was that I didn't have to endure those anymore. I reached up and plucked a bud from one of the branches and twirled it between my fingers. I didn't need a stick to reach anymore. These trees seemed almost small to me now. I thought of my sister and wondered, as I'd done a million times before, what she would be doing now had she lived. She would probably be standing here with me now, as we said goodbye to our grandmother. Instead, she was beneath me in the cold ground. I smelled the apple bud, kissed it and dropped it as I walked away.

Chapter Four

I approached the farmhouse slowly, soaking it all in. It struck me how different the reality of it was compared to the memory of it I'd held in my head. The orchard felt almost unchanged. I expected the house to appear that way, too. I wasn't sure why I thought a house and its surroundings wouldn't age. It was either that, or my brain just wouldn't compute that the good parts of this place could be any different than before I left.

When I walked inside though, that all got tossed out, because the interior of the house looked exactly as I'd left it. It was almost eerie, like entering a time capsule. The same sheer organdy curtains specked with little flowers and ruffled trim still hung on the big south-facing picture window. The sturdy oak table remained planted firmly in the dining room, with six chairs pushed in around it, even though there had only been four of us, and that was when my mother had been here, which occurred only rarely. Even the bookshelf with all of my homeschooling books remained.

The reference shelf, as Grammy referred to it, was a modest bookcase along the back wall of the living room, which held a set of *Encyclopedia Britannica* books, several old copies of the *Farmer's Almanac*, and a *Webster's Dictionary* thicker than the width of one of my arms. Grammy often referred me to this shelf as if it contained all of the answers to the universe. It was all I had as a child, and though I'd pretty much consumed all of the words contained within the pages of those dated books, I still sought answers that were not to be found here.

I recalled vividly working on an assignment one day that referenced something about twins. I was probably all of ten and I stopped reading and called out to Grammy who was behind the butcher block counter cooking.

"What does fraternal mean?" I had asked her.

"That's a very good question," she'd said. "Maybe you should check the dictionary on the reference shelf."

The dictionary defined not only the word "fraternal," but also specifically "fraternal twins," which it stated were *a set—though not resembling one another, which developed from two individual fertilized ova.*

"I'm confused," I told her. "If me and Sonny weren't alike, why does everyone say we were twins?"

"You and your sister were in your mom's tummy together, but you were hatched from two different eggs, not the same egg."

"Was our mother a chicken?"

She'd laughed. "No. Your mother was and still is your mother."

I wasn't sure if that had solved anything for me because I wanted to say that it felt more like Grammy was my mom, but I didn't. Even at a fairly young age, I'd figured out roughly how things worked…at least in my family. It was best not to ask too many questions, especially when it came to my mom. Where she was and what she was doing was not of my concern. Grammy tried to sugarcoat the troubles, both my mother's and my own. And GG ignored that they were happening altogether. And that was why I'd never gotten treatment for my panic attacks. Because what is not talked about does not exist in the Andersen family. It was also why eventually the bubble had to burst because trouble like ours didn't disappear; it grew and pressurized, and with nowhere to go, it eventually exploded.

I slowly moved through the house letting my mind go to the places from my childhood memories. Outside the kitchen window, I could see the old tire GG had hung from the huge silver maple out the back. Next to that was the vegetable garden where they planted things just for the family, like tomatoes, carrots, cucumbers, and the like. It looked as if it hadn't even been tilled this season, which made perfect sense because Grammy usually tended to the veggies.

In the living room, I thought of all the times I stayed up late, sitting on the old plaid sofa and watching TV. I envisioned Grammy with an apron pulled over her house dress, though never tied in the back, standing at the butcher block counter rolling out dough, or bent over the kitchen table helping me with my schoolwork.

Upstairs, I peeked into my old bedroom and I wasn't at all shocked to see that Grammy hadn't touched it much. The room, like the rest of the house, was exactly as I remembered it. A single bed with a metal frame took up most of the small room. A rocking chair and dresser filled the rest of it. I hadn't been a typical girlie girl. There were no posters of pop singers or flowery pillows. I kept all of my artwork in a sketch pad that had been tucked into my top dresser drawer growing up. That was it. Simple. No frills. The only décor was a blanket, a brightly colored afghan that Grammy had stitched. It was still there, folded over the back of the rocker.

Across the hall, the door to my mother's bedroom

was slightly open, and though I knew I shouldn't, I peeked in. I expected it to be altered, but it followed suit from everything else and looked more or less the same. This did surprise me. Taking it all in, I hadn't realized until now how young the décor felt. The single bed had a light-blue quilt with a ruffled duster on it, and the curtains were light yellow with white stripes. A stuffed animal was propped up on the pillow. If I hadn't known better, I'd have thought a girl of eight slept in this room, not a woman of forty-eight.

Deep down, I knew I should be saddened by this revelation. My mother's mental health had been stunted by the tragedy of losing a child after all, but even now, I couldn't get over the fact that I was also her child, and I was still here, yet she didn't seem to care about that at all. I closed the door and started to head back downstairs, but just before the steps, Grammy and GG's door was wide open, so I stopped and stood in the threshold and inhaled the scent of Grammy's perfume. It poured out as if inviting me in.

On a little table next to GG's reading chair, I spotted a stack of envelopes. I smiled, knowing exactly what they were. Before I left for college, he'd made me promise to write to him. He wasn't a phone or a computer guy. He was a farmer who still believed in communicating the old-fashioned way, through the good-ole United States Postal Service. I held up that promise. To my surprise, he even wrote back to me on occasion. Most of his letters were short and sweet, often talking about the weather, how the crops were fairing, maybe a quick note about his aching back or feet. Getting those letters had been soothing to my soul those first years away from home.

I glanced over at Grammy's side of the room, my eyes welling with tears. Next to the lamp on her night table was a perfectly folded silk hanky. I tiptoed over to it as if I were a child again, and what I was doing was forbidden. I picked up the hanky and held it to my nose, taking in more of her essence. It was pristine white with a lavender embroidered edging. It looked as though it had never been touched, except maybe by a hot iron. In the upper right-hand corner were Grammy's initials. She'd clearly monogrammed the gold lettering herself. The hand embroidery gave it just the perfect amount of imperfection. It read: IDA. Grammy's first name was also the abbreviation for her full name: Ida Dee Andersen. I considered using the hanky to wipe away my tears, but I didn't want to sully it, so I set it back down the way I'd found it wishing Grammy would be able to return to it, but knowing that was impossible.

****

Back downstairs, I made GG something to eat, but he still hadn't come inside, even though he'd promised that he would. I was fully expecting it, as this had been a constant source of frustration for my grandma while I was growing up. GG never stopped fidgeting. I was pretty sure he thought that if he quit moving, he would die. It didn't make a ton of sense because his own father was the same way, and he had a heart attack in the middle of the field one day. Whatever the reasoning GG had for it, he rarely took a break of any sort and we often didn't see him until dinner was on the table and Grammy went out on the porch and whistled with both hands stuck in her mouth. I could never do it, so on those occasions when she sent me to call him in, I always had to run around the property like a chicken with my head cut off yelling his name. I never found him in the same spot.

Much like then, I went back out and hunted for him on the property. As I roamed, I kept my eyes peeled for Max. I knew he had to be around somewhere. An unfamiliar car was parked near the pole barn in his normal parking spot. It wasn't the same car he'd had ten years ago, but I was sure it was his.

He'd been GG's main farm hand since I was a young girl. And that's how I came to be friends with his son. Brad often tagged along with Max in the summer or on days off of school. He went to the public school in the next town over. And since I was farm schooled after third grade, I was always here. Brad was supposed to be helping his dad when he tagged along, but he didn't care much for the work, so he and I often ended up goofing around somewhere on the property. And when we got older, when we were both tasked with chores we didn't want to do, we would hide up on the hill together to get out of the constant hassle of farm work.

Wandering the edges of the property line still in search of GG, I came to the red shed. My blood began to boil the second I saw it. The red shed was nothing more than a small shack GG had built out of torn-down barn wood shortly after my mother came back from a long absence from the farm. She called it her artist loft even though there was no loft and she wasn't an artist. At least I'd never seen her do anything of the sort. She had gone to the University of Minnesota to pursue a degree in art before Sonny and I were born, but by her second semester, she was pregnant with us and she quit school and took the waitressing job.

I had no idea what kind of artistic endeavors took place within those four walls, though I had long-held suspicions there was nothing creative going on at all. I simply couldn't picture my mother sculpting, drawing, painting, or any such thing. I assumed the shed was the place she went to be away from the rest of us, me in particular. It was her private sanctuary complete with a heavy padlock on the door. To say that I resented the red shed was an understatement.

One morning, at the height of my teen angst, when my hatred toward my absentee mother was at the height of my breaking point, I set off to bust into the red shed. I'd planned it all out and even gone so far as to go into GGs tool cabinet and borrow his bolt cutter after consulting with Brad about what I needed to beat the lock on the door.

I wasn't allowed inside. This fact had been made incredibly clear to me over the years. I could knock if I needed my mother, but that was it. That day, her car was not parked in the driveway. I knew she was not inside the shed. I had turned in a full circle in front of the door and when I didn't see a living soul around, I had taken a cautious step toward the padlock.

I wasn't sure what I was expecting to see inside, but it felt big, like unlocking the shed would unlock my mother's deepest, darkest thoughts. If I could just see what she was hiding, maybe I could understand her better. Seconds from finding out what made my mother tick, an unfamiliar voice had boomed from behind. "Luna!"

I'd whipped around to see GG standing there. I hadn't recognized the voice as belonging to my grandfather because he'd never called me Luna before and I'd felt it deep within me. It hurt. It was the worst form of punishment he could unleash upon me.

Our eyes locked and he followed up with, "Get yourself away from there right now, young lady!"

I saw the disappointment in my grandpa's face, and my heart couldn't take it, so I ran. We never discussed it after, and I never attempted to break into the red shed again. Until now.

Today, approaching it, I felt the déjà vu soaking into my skin, but when I reached the padlock, something was different. The rusty clasp that usually stayed flush with the wall, securing it with the big metal Master lock, was flapping in the wind. A small gap allowed me to see sunlight pouring into the space. I took another tentative step, reached out to push the door open, when—

"Lu?"

This time I knew it was GG without turning to look, but I did anyway. He was standing a good distance away. He hadn't raised his voice in anger this time. He'd only yelled out so I could hear him in the breeze.

"Yeah?" I said, searching his old eyes.

"I'm heading inside. You coming?"

"Okay, yeah. I'm coming."

He nodded. I watched him to see if he'd walk away, but he stood waiting, so I yielded and started toward him with my head hanging down, not unlike when I was younger. Something else was similar to the previous time GG pulled me away from this spot: I was still clueless as to what mysteries lay concealed behind the rotting barn slats of the red shed. It seemed I was destined to never find out the contents of the small structure and thus continued to be equally mystified by my own mother.

Back inside, GG examined the ham sandwich I'd prepared for him. He grunted. "No butter?"

"On ham?"

"Gram always butters my bread."

"Oh. Sorry."

I got up to grab the butter from the fridge, but he said, "Never mind. I don't need it."

I got it anyway, but he didn't spread any on. We finished eating in silence.

Chapter Five

GG insisted that we drive the truck back to the hospital instead of my rental car. It was the same green Ford pickup he'd had since I was a little girl. His prize possession. He babied it more than pretty much anything else I could think of, constantly washing and waxing it, changing the oil and other fluids. It was the only car he ever made room for in his garage. The garage would have had plenty of space for two more cars, but GG was a supreme packrat of the highest order. He even admitted it. He hated to toss things. Why should he? He argued. With all of this space? And you never knew when you might need a lid to a pan you no longer were in possession of, an empty shoe box, a piece of rope cut from a package. He kept it all. He blamed it on the Great Depression but he was a little too young for that. Whatever the reason, he had managed to fill two of the three stalls in the garage with boxes of junk, old furniture, tools, and all sorts of other unless items. But his truck, well, she was worth making space for. Everyone else had to park in the driveway.

I couldn't believe the old pickup was still running, though it was probably because GG had taken such good care of it throughout the years. He wasn't technically supposed to drive anymore. He'd failed his last eye test at the DMV and refused to retake it. He had too much pride. Grammy had been hiding his keys for the last few

34

years, much to his great displeasure. Even when he was still driving, he'd pretty much stuck close to home, so he never put on many miles.

I'd learned to drive in this very truck with GG instructing me, so it felt surreal to be behind the wheel again with him next to me in the passenger seat, as if time hadn't budged. I half expected him to beg me to let him drive, because I knew my mother wasn't having it, and I probably would have let him to be honest, but he didn't ask. His heart probably wasn't in it right now. I think he was just happy to be in the old girl again, because he seemed to be more awake on the quick jaunt back to the hospital than he'd been on the trip to the house. Either that, or the simple act of being back on the farm had rejuvenated his spirit. It definitely had mine.

When we returned to the hospital, everything was the same as before we'd left, except there was a man I didn't recognize sitting in the chair opposite my mother. At first, I thought maybe it was Max, but this man did not have a cowboy hat on his head. In fact, his head had nothing on it, including hair. Once I realized it wasn't Max, and upon second look, I realized I didn't know this person at all in my Grammy's hospital room, but it didn't take long for me to figure out who he must be. A new boyfriend.

"Luna," my mother said, "This is Ernest."

"You can call me Ernie," he said.

I wanted to say that I wouldn't be calling him anything because he wouldn't be around long enough, but I didn't. Instead, I forced a polite, "Hello."

I wondered to myself what number boyfriend this one was in the long chain of men my mom had somehow managed to whittle together over the years. I was actually surprised there were still men in Alton who my mother hadn't dated at one point or another. She didn't seem to have a hard time attracting them. Even at almost fifty, she was a good looking woman. Her light brown hair was long and full-bodied. Her skin was smooth and flawless. She was tall and in really good shape, probably better than I was. For all of her other issues, she somehow managed to keep herself looking fairly well put together in terms of her clothing and appearance. Physically, she wasn't a bad catch. The problem was that once she was caught, it didn't take long for men to realize she wasn't a keeper, and they would quickly release her again into the wild shortly thereafter. Because on the inside, she was too damaged even for the most patient human. Since Sonny's death, she was prone to bouts of delusions that caused her to have irrational tantrums. It was likely some type of PTSD and chronic depression. The only person who was ever able to get her to calm down while in the throes of madness and chaos was Grammy, because my mother didn't listen to anyone else. And Grammy could be stern and a bit scary when she needed to be. She had never been that to me. She had been the exact opposite. She was lovely and affectionate, a teacher, a friend, someone who nurtured me and told me as often as she could that she loved me while holding me in a tight bear hug.

As I sat looking at my dying grandmother now, I worried about what might happen to my mother in the wake of Grammy's passing. Even I didn't have what it took to keep my mother stable. If anything, I triggered her, and her me. I wanted to be loving and supporting of her, I truly did. It wasn't her fault, what had happened to cause her to be this way. According to Grammy, my mother had watched my twin sister get killed. Grammy said that it wasn't something a mother could come back from, and though my mom seemed to progressively get better over the years, she still suffered from the occasional episode that would pull her down into the murky waters that took anyone and everything near to her into the deep, dark abyss. She was a strong force to reckon with and I was exactly the opposite. Though I often asked direct questions, I backed down on a dime when challenged.

So, while I thought these invisible character traits made it unfair to the men my mother kept bringing home, she clearly disagreed because Ernie was proof of this. The thing that annoyed me most about this one was that I hadn't been told about him. I understood why though. Grammy was the one to keep me informed about the plethora of rotating boyfriends, not my mother herself. And GG kept out of it entirely, so he was no help when it came to any of this. It concerned me to the point that since arriving, I hadn't stopped wondering not only who would take care of my mother, but also who would be there to look after GG? Because my mom was anything but reliable and while she loved her dad, I did not think she had what it took to take care of him. She couldn't even look after herself. And bringing a boyfriend to the hospital was proof of that very fact. All of these things suddenly seemed to fall on my shoulders. The heavy weight of what I needed to do, without Grammy there to guide me, was overwhelming.

Ernie looked like a perfectly nice and normal guy. If only my mother was nice and normal as well. His shirt was tucked in and he had on a pair of clean jeans. Sure, he was bald, but he had a kind-looking face and patient eyes. He'd need more than his sight to be able to deal with my mother's issues, and those eyes needed more patience than all of the monks in a monastery if they wanted to put up with the unpredictable moodiness that my mother brought to a relationship. His glasses didn't look thick enough for that.

"I'm going to step out for some fresh air," my mother declared, getting up from her seat.

GG, who hadn't even bothered to sit down yet, turned and followed behind her. I knew it was too hard for him to be cooped up in this small room with Grammy like this. I watched them go, expecting Ernie to jump onto the exiting train, but he stayed in his chair, or rather, my chair. I sat down in Mom's seat and focused on Grammy, hoping to have a little time to be alone with her. I knew she couldn't talk, but maybe her strong will would somehow rub off on me.

He turned to me and said, "Jenny tells me that you live in New York City."

I gave an internal eye roll. This small fact held so much intrigue to people from Alton, Minnesota. "I do."

"Whereabouts?"

"In the East Village."

"Oh, yeah? I used to live on the Upper East Side."

"Really?"

"Yep. I went out there to go to college. NYU. I had big dreams of getting a business degree and working in the corporate world, but it didn't take me long to realize it wasn't for me."

"No?"

"Nope. Too many phonies."

"I went to NYU, too."

He nodded. "Your mom mentioned that. What do

you do now?"

"I work in advertising. I do some freelance illustrating on the side for children's books and occasionally magazines."

"Ah, an artist, like your mom."

"Yeah. Something like that," I said. "What do you do?"

"I'm a paramedic."

"Oh, yeah?"

"Uh huh. A proud member of the Alton Upper Valley Unit."

"That's cool. So, how did you and my mom meet?"

"We went to high school together."

"Ah."

That made some sense. It meant he knew mom before the B.S. or Before Sonny was killed. I had no idea what my mother was like back then, but it had to have been better than now. My early memories of her, before we came to live at the farm, have a neutral feel in my brain. I recall bits and pieces of our time in the apartment, and also of me and my sister being watched by the old neighbor lady down the hall when Mom was at work, but it all felt like a hazy dream.

Not only did I often wonder what things would have been different if Sonny had lived, but in particular, I wondered about my mother. Would she have been an upstanding single parent? Would she have shown us unrepressed love? Been nurturing? I would have even tolerated a small attempt at any of these things. Instead, what I ended up with was a mother who kept her distance, let her parents raise me, and did everything she could to keep me in the dark right along with her.

****

Later, Mom and Ernie were sitting together out in the waiting area and GG and I were planted on a small sofa in Grammy's room. The sun was going down outside the window. It was quiet except for the monitors and our thoughts. I'd already looked at my phone and all of the magazines that were available to me while GG just stared straight ahead with a Styrofoam cup of coffee in his hands.

"GG?" I finally asked him.

"Mmmm?"

"What do you think of Ernie?"

He shrugged his shoulders.

"Because, and I'm kind of shocked I'm saying this, but I kind of like him."

GG turned and looked at me. Besides the extreme exhaustion on his face, he managed to raise his brow in question.

"It's just…have you ever felt the need to take one of Mom's boyfriends aside and be honest with them? Explain to them how she is? Because I was talking to Ernie earlier and he seemed so put together, smart even. I—"

"He knows," GG said, interrupting my struggle to formulate my thoughts about my mom in a polite manner. It was hardly something we discussed out loud.

"What?"

"Ernie knows all about your mother."

"He does? How?"

"He's been a paramedic in this town for a long time now. He's been on calls…when we had to have people come out to the farm…during particularly bad episodes. When your grandma and I couldn't restrain her. When she needed more help than we could give her. Ernie was

40

there more than once. He witnessed it. Once he even talked her down from the hay loft when we couldn't."

"And…he's still…interested in her?"

GG shrugged again. "She's been doing better lately."

I nodded, and GG turned and sank down into the couch a bit deeper. He took his brown stocking cap off and set it on his lap. I was surprised to see that he still had a little bit of brown hair on the top of his head.

I knew what GG said was true; she did seem to be doing better, but there had been other periods where we thought, hoped, prayed, that all of the troubles were behind us, and it turned out to not last. Though my own issues were nowhere as severe as my mothers, I didn't trust myself to put such a large burden on someone else, which was why I was nearing thirty and still single. It didn't seem right to me, knowing what I was like, worried that it could progress, that a partner might have to deal with all of that down the road. Sure, I'd dated, but I always kept it casual. My mother kept trying to pursue something more lasting, concrete. I had no idea why. I guess maybe she thought it would fix her. A more sane person would have figured out by now that all it ever seemed to do was complicate things further. My mother never learned from her mistakes. I liked Ernie. He seemed different from most of the other guys Mom had set her sights on, which had me utterly baffled by his intentions, but I figured just like all of the other men who had come before him, he'd eventually figure out that a long-term relationship with my mother was unsustainable and he'd move on. I suppose it wasn't my place to dictate my mother's love life at this point, though I would likely be here to deal with picking up the pieces when it went to pot.

When I looked back over at GG, his eyes were closed. I got up quietly, took the cup from his hand, and grabbed the blanket hanging over the edge of the armrest, unfolded it, and spread it over my grandfather without disturbing his slumber.

I sat back down in the chair next to my grammy's bed and I held her hand for a while in the darkening room. I had no idea how any of us were going to make it without her, but we had no choice in the matter. She was slipping further away with each beep of the slowing heart monitor.

When my mother stepped in the room again, I quickly wiped at my wet cheeks.

"I'll take over," she said to me. "Why don't you go and get some sleep."

"What about GG?"

"He'll be fine sleeping on that sofa tonight."

I nodded and headed back to the hotel across the street.

Chapter Six

Ending up at Finley and Son's Bar hadn't been my intention when I got in GG's pickup, but it wasn't yet nine o'clock, and though I was wiped out from the emotional toll of the day, I knew I wasn't going to be able to sleep. I was planning to just take a drive around town before going back to the hotel, but as I passed by, the lure of the old biker bar was too strong. Or maybe it was the liquor inside of it. Either way, I parked and went in.

The air circulating was stagnant, like the rest of the town. There were a few more patrons than the previous night, but it did nothing to change the depressing and lonely vibe. I saw immediately that Brad wasn't behind the bar. I wanted to believe I wasn't disappointed, but it was hard to lie to myself. I was hoping to see him again. Instead, the server from the night before stood in his place behind the taps.

I sat down at the same stool I'd taken the night before, making it clear I was already establishing a small town pattern. Thankfully, I wouldn't be here long enough to make a true habit of it. An old man wearing a brown pleather jacket, maybe a bit younger than GG, occupied the seat to my left. Now, he appeared to be a regular if I'd ever seen one. He looked too comfortable with these sad surroundings. A dark lager was half gone from the pint glass in front of him. He nodded when I sat down, but then went back to looking at his phone.

When the bartender came to take my order, I saw that up close she was maybe not quite as young as I'd suspected the night prior, though she was possibly more attractive than I'd been able to discern from the distance of the darkened room. I wanted to dislike her, but I had no reason to, especially since she gave off an immediate friendly vibe that was more sincere than I would have expected for a bartender in a small town bar.

"Hey there," she said. "You were here last night right? Brad's friend from out of town?"

I nodded. "That's me."

"Well, unfortunately, Brad isn't here right now. He has the night off, but whatever you're having, it's on me. I think you were drinking an Uncle Mickey last night, right?"

"An Uncle Mickey?"

"Oh, a Hart's."

"Actually, you know what? I think I'll try the local IPA tonight instead."

"Good choice. I'll be right back."

An Uncle Mickey? Why did they call it that? I considered asking her, but I thought I probably knew. That must have been what Mickey drank when they first started up the bar because that was the same stuff that Brad always seemed to have when we went to bonfires at the beach or when we hung out on the hill. It was a cheap, light beer that was canned locally in St. Paul. It made sense.

As I nursed my drink, I peered over at the Finley family photo again, wondering what it was about Mickey that felt so familiar to me. All I could think was that I'd probably met him at some point when I was little and just didn't remember exactly when. Since our families were so connected, I'd been dragged to all sorts of various events ranging from BBQs, weddings, and funerals to graduation parties over the years. I wondered when Mickey had made his escape from Alton. I made a note to ask Brad about dates just to quell my own curiosity.

The old man next to me set his phone down on the bar and looked at me for an awkward amount of time. "You're not from around here," he declared. He'd obviously overheard the bartender say I was from out of town, so I thought I'd have a little fun with him.

"Born and raised," I said.

He moved his face closer and gave me a skeptical once over. "Haven't seen you before," he said, still studying my face intently, because townies were always sure they knew every single person who'd ever lived in Alton. When he didn't make any connections, he was at a loss. I could have told him that I was an Andersen, or Gus and Ida's granddaughter, or from Andersen's Farm on Upper Alton Road, or even Jenny Andersen's daughter and he would have known, but I realized I wasn't in the mood to get into any of my family's history, because it was another reason why I often loathed this town. My mom's reputation often preceded her, even when I was a little girl. I remember hearing people in town whisper things in the grocery store or the gas station. *"That's Jenny's Andersen's daughter." "The one she gave up."* Or, *"The one whose sister was killed." "Just heartbreaking, really. Isn't it? Poor girl."*

I just never knew what people might say about us. It was often pity, but sometimes it was worse. And while I harbored some bad feelings toward my mother, it didn't always sit with me when strangers did. Nope. I let the conversation die. Getting into it with a stranger in a bar wasn't on my agenda this evening.

When the bartender came back with another drink for him, he said to her, "How're the kids?"

"They're really good. Tanner's playing soccer and Elise started piano lessons."

"How old are they now?" he asked.

"Elise is five and Tanner just turned eight."

The old man shook his head in disbelief. "Goes fast, doesn't it? I can't believe I have grandkids older than that now."

"Yeah, Martha was in here a few nights ago showing off pictures. That Dillon is gonna be a heartbreaker when he gets older. He's a real cutie."

They both laughed. She glanced at me and probably saw me staring at her, trying to process the fact that she had two kids. "Can I get you another beer?" she asked.

"No, thanks. I'm good."

She nodded and headed back to the other side of the bar. I turned to the old guy. "She doesn't look old enough to have an eight-year-old child."

He chuckled. "That family has good genes."

"Which family is that?" I asked.

"The Finley family."

"She's a Finley?"

"Yeah. She's Kenny's youngest daughter."

"You're kidding! That's Kelsey?"

"That's her."

Kelsey Finley was the most popular girl in town when I was a kid. She was the most popular girl in all of the neighboring towns, too. I didn't even go to the public school and even I knew that. She probably didn't recognize me, just as the old man had no idea who I was.

I'd been sheltered high in the Alton hills by my own fears growing up. I hadn't realized who Kelsey was because I think the last time we'd seen one another, I was probably in my early teens. She was a few years older than me and Brad, but she seemed so much more mature at the time. She was gorgeous then, so it made sense that she would still be. It also meant I'd been very wrong about her flirting with Brad last night because Kelsey and Brad were cousins, and obviously, they were now business partners, having both taken over a family share of this bar from their dads.

After I finished my drink, I left some cash on the bar and headed out. Just rounding on ten o'clock when I stepped outside, it was darker outside than I expected it to be, and I stood digging around in my bag in the parking lot trying to find the keys to the truck with only the light of one flickering street lamp nearby when a low rumble of thunder moved high through the atmosphere. I looked up and saw the dark clouds hurling toward me. The black sky made sense now. A storm was coming. I suddenly felt the charge in the air.

A few quick flashes of lightning gave me enough to see by and I was able to fish the keys from my bag. I put them in the truck's ignition and twisted it. The engine whined but did not turn over. "Shit."

I tried again, this time giving the old girl a little gas as I did. It had always worked for GG, but I wasn't GG and the truck probably sensed it. He always called her Old Girl, like it was the truck's name. He also talked to her like she was an old friend. I was desperate, so the next time I tried turning it over, I said, "Come on Old Girl. You can do this." After another failed attempt, I took a more aggressive approach. "Start, you old piece of junk, or I'll take you to the garbage dump!" That didn't seem to work either. I repeated the process a few more times before I stopped, not wanting to flood the engine.

Unwilling to call my mother to come and get me, but not having another plan, I sat in the truck waiting, hoping that if I tried again in a few minutes, there would be a spark. That was all I needed. Just one little spark. I did not want to have to call Jenny. Anything but that. The wind started to pick up speed and I felt oddly vulnerable sitting in a parking lot in a pick-up truck. I knew I had to do something because I couldn't just keep talking to myself hoping for a miracle, but I couldn't come up with a course of action that didn't involve my mother, therefore, I was at a standstill. I put my head down on the steering wheel and listened to the wind and what I thought was more rumbles of thunder off in the distance.

When I lifted my head up though, I realized it wasn't thunder at all, but a car pulling in. Headlights cut through the darkness and stop directly behind the truck. It sent a chill up my spine because there were ample other places to park in the barren wasteland of the large, empty concrete jungle. Why were they choosing to park right next to me, of all places? I wasn't even particularly close to the door. I reached over and pushed both locks down. The Old Girl was so old that they were still manual buttons.

I looked in the rearview mirror, but the beam from the other headlights was so bright in comparison to the surrounding blackness, it blinded me. I heard the car door slam, but the headlights continued to make it impossible for me to see anything. The car idled while footsteps approached. I turned to the window and squinted. I could just make out a silhouette of someone standing outside my door. All I could see was the shape of a man. A man wearing a cowboy hat. I cranked the window down.

"Max?"

Chapter Seven

"Luna?" he said, bending to my level. "Is that you?"

"Yeah. It's me!"

"I was driving by and saw Gus's truck in the lot, which was…unusual, but now it makes sense."

"It won't start," I told him just as heavy raindrops began pelting the windshield.

"I can take you back, if you want."

"That would be great. Thanks."

I grabbed my bag and the keys and jumped out. Max and I sprinted back to his car to avoid a total soaking. When we slammed the doors, the sky opened up. Rain and small hail pinged off the vehicle making it too loud to converse as we rode up the winding hills.

I knew Max was taking me to the farm and I didn't argue with him because my rental car was still there, so it made the most sense. I wasn't sure if Mom would be there when I got there or if I'd be staying in the old house alone. I wasn't sure which of those two options scared me more.

"How have you been?" Max asked once the rain let up a bit.

"Not too bad. You?"

"Yeah. Okay." He paused. "Been meaning to get to the hospital. How's everybody holding up? How's Ida?"

"The doctor said it's probably a matter of days," I said, somehow managing the words, knowing I wouldn't have tried if it had been anyone but Max beside me.

He cleared his throat. "It's never easy, but the slowness of it is almost worse, I imagine."

"It's not fun."

"If I don't make it down there, please give my regards," he said. "Me and hospitals don't really go together well."

I nodded, understanding.

"Brad tending bar tonight? You run into him yet?"

"He was there last night," I said.

"I bet he was happy to see you," he said.

I wasn't sure how to answer that. "Hey, can I ask you something? I saw a picture of you and your brothers on the wall. Your brother Mickey…was he still around when I was a kid? He looks sort of familiar to me."

"Mick? No. He left Alton well before you were born, shortly after the big break up."

"Big break up?"

Max turned his head toward me for a split second. "Mickey and Jenny. You didn't know?"

"Mickey and my mom dated?"

"Yeah. It was their senior year of high school. They were…pretty serious. I think Mick thought they were going to get married or something, and then Jenny told him she was leaving for college. He didn't take it well."

"And that's why he left? Brad told me he left Alton under mysterious circumstances and nobody really knew why."

"As far as I know. We never really talked about it outright, but, yeah. I think that was it. Your mom broke his heart."

That was a shocker. One I was still processing when Max turned into the driveway. There were no lights on inside the house and I remembered that I had no key. "Do you know if the spare key is still under the porch swing?" I asked as Max stopped the car in front of the house.

"Should be. Gus staying at the hospital?"

"Yeah. And I have no idea if Mom will come back tonight or not."

Max nodded. "I'll wait to make sure you get in."

"Thanks. And thank you for the rescue."

"Anytime. It's nice to see you, even under the circumstances." He patted my leg and smiled, just like an uncle might do, which was exactly how I thought of him, and now I wondered if there was a good reason for it.

"Good night, Max," I said, jumping out.

"Night, Luna."

I sprinted the few steps to the porch. Max's headlights lit up the swing enough for me to see the outline of it. I reached under and swept my hand along the bottom feeling for the metal box GG had attached when I got my driver's license and was always forgetting my key, ringing the doorbell, waking everyone up at night when I got home late. My finger made contact with the metal Hide-A-Key box and I slid it open, catching the key in the palm of my other hand when it dropped down. I held it up to show Max. In response, he put the car in reverse and backed down the gravel driveway as I unlocked the front door of the farmhouse.

Inside, I turned on a lamp in the living room and plopped down on the old plaid couch, listening to the storm roll through. There was nothing like the sound of a good spring thunderstorm in the country. It didn't sound the same in the middle of a huge metropolitan area while housed in the interior of an apartment complex. I laid my head down on one of the couch pillows Grammy had sewn years ago. As I started to drift off, I couldn't help but ponder the information Max had dropped on me. I wasn't sure why it surprised me so much that Mom had dated a Finley. It even explained why she and Max had always seemed to hold one another at an uncomfortable distance. I guess the thing that did shock me was that it was my mom who had apparently broken things off while it sounded like Mickey had wanted the relationship to continue on. That wasn't my mom's usual dating pattern, not since Sonny died, anyway. What could have made her change course in such an extreme manner?

****

I had no idea what time it was when a loud banging woke me. It was obviously morning because the sun was already blasting through the sheer curtains that hung on the front bay windows. When I realized it was someone on the front porch, I peeked through the curtain on the door to see who was knocking at such an ungodly hour.

"Morning," Brad said. He looked wide awake and smelled clean, like he'd just showered. I couldn't tell if his hair was wet because it was covered by a baseball cap. He had on some outdoorsy hiking pants, sneakers, and a hoodie, and he cradled a glass casserole dish in his arms. "Did I wake you?"

"No," I lied.

He thrust a covered dish toward me. "Sherry made this for you."

I didn't know who Sherry was, but I took it. "Thank you. Do you want to come in?"

"Actually, I was thinking...you wanna take a hike up to the hill?"

"Now?"

53

"Why not? It's a nice day."

I guess this explained his hiking pants. I looked at my watch. It was 8:00 a.m. I hadn't pegged Brad as a morning guy. "Let me just set the dish inside."

I left the door cracked open as I went in. I ducked into the half-bath just off of the kitchen upon my return to splash some water on my face and try to fix my matted hair as best I could. I'd slept in my clothes because I hadn't been anticipating sleeping at the farm in the first place. Luckily, Brad hadn't seen me yesterday, so he likely assumed that I'd already been up and dressed.

"I'm ready," I said, returning to the porch and found him sitting on the old swing.

The air was crisp and held a good bit of moisture from the storm, but there were plenty of crunchy leaves left over from fall for my street shoes to find some traction as we headed up to the highest point on the property. Back in the day, the hill seemed much steeper than it appeared to me now, but it was still a little bit of a jaunt.

Once we reached the peak, it didn't take but a minute to find our spot, the one that had a clear view for miles. "Wow," I whispered more to myself than to Brad. "The view is just as stunning as I remembered."

"It's pretty spectacular," he agreed. "It's been a while since I've been up here."

We surveyed the rows of cornfields below which had been planted earlier in the spring and had only short stalks visible at this point in the season. It allowed us to see much of the valley below with the rolling green hills leading to the river peeking out from the east in the distance.

Brad and I had spent hours there together as kids,

mostly talking, but sometimes we'd do other things too. It was around my sixteenth birthday when he brought a six pack of cheap beer and we spread a blanket on the ground, hidden away in the grove of trees. It was dusk and the bugs were eating us alive, but we stayed there until it was well past dark.

He handed me a can of Hart's like it was a perfectly normal occurrence. And maybe it was for him, but for a girl who didn't go to public school and who lived with her grandparents, it wasn't. GG smoked a pipe, but I'd never seen him drink. He said farmers didn't have time for that. I'd never observed Grammy drink alcohol either. My mother probably had, but not in my presence which was most of the time.

Brad cracked his open and began to slurp it. I didn't want to look like it was my first time, so I tried to be as nonchalant about it as I could. I sipped slowly as we talked about random stuff. Brad's mom and baby sister had been in a horrific car accident when he was five. His mother had died on impact, but his little sister, Addy, had held on for several weeks before Max had to make the terrible decision to let her go. So, Brad and I had shared experience in that department—both of our sisters had been killed and we each lacked a mother, or in my case, a mother-figure. We didn't often talk about those things, but they were unspoken threads that weaved in and around our words. No matter how mundane the conversation was, these burdens were always there, sitting heavy on our minds. We were so in tune, it was like we could read each other's thoughts. Talking to him, even about nothing, always made me feel better about my circumstances.

That night, Brad kissed me for the first time, but it

felt so strange. I wasn't sure if it was because it was a little like I was kissing my brother, or if it was because shortly after it began, I had the most intense panic attack I'd ever experienced. It had all the usual characteristics of my standard attacks—the sudden dizziness, a sense of things closing in around me, my chest tightening—but it was also somehow different.

I couldn't say for sure how long I was down in it, but when I came out of the murky trance, I remembered Brad waving his hand in front of my face, saying, "Luna? Are you okay?"

"Yeah."

"What happened?"

I felt so stupid. I didn't tell Brad about my troubles that day or any other. I was already an odd kid, a social outcast. He was the only one who treated me like I was normal. I didn't want to be a freak, especially not to him. "I-I'm not sure," I'd managed to sputter.

I could see from his expression that he thought I was rejecting him and his kiss, so I added, "I honestly just think…I might be drunk."

Brad's dejected expression broke all at once, and he laughed wholeheartedly. I was relieved, and yet he never tried to kiss me again after that. My confusion surrounding the whole situation stayed with me like the aftertaste from the cheap beer.

Ten years later, I could sense Brad reading my thoughts. "Remember how we would avoid our chores and hide up here?"

"Yeah."

"Those were good times," he said. "Also, weird times."

"Yeah."

"Remember when we kissed?"

"I was just thinking about that," I said.

"God," he said, shaking his head.

I watched his expression, but couldn't get a read. Desperate to know, I blurted out the question I'd been pondering. "Why didn't you ever kiss me again after that?"

"Because you made it pretty clear that you weren't into it...or me, so..."

"It wasn't that," I said. "It was something else."

"Something else? What?"

"I...had a panic attack. It had nothing to do with...what happened between us." I sighed. "I started having them when I was in second or third grade. It was the reason I stopped going to public school."

He stifled a laugh. "Well, if my kissing you caused you to have a panic attack, then I still think the message reads the same."

"No! It wasn't you! I promise. It's this place. It's...I don't know exactly what, but whatever it was, moving away made the attacks stop."

His eyes widened. "Moving away from me made the attacks stop?"

"Not you! I started having them before we were...close."

"When did they start?" he said.

"The first one happened when I was having a playdate with a friend from grade school. We were playing hide and seek and I hid under a blanket."

Brad gave me a weird look.

"What?" I said.

"That was me."

"No, it wasn't. It was Fia Butcher, the redheaded girl

I was friends with from my second grade class."

"I was there, too," he said. "In fact, it was me, not Fia, who found you hidden under the blanket. You were sort of quivering. I thought you were having a seizure at first."

"Really? I have…no memory of that."

He took a step toward the edge of the hill away from me and crossed his arms around his chest. I reached out and touched his shoulder. "Brad, I'm serious. It's not you."

"What is it then?" he asked, swinging back around to look at me.

"I really don't know."

"You had one the other night, didn't you? At the bar? When you saw me."

"Yeah, I did."

"See?"

"Well, it doesn't really matter anyway. I mean…you're with Sherry now, right?"

His face crinkled up. "Sherry?"

"The woman who made the hot dish you brought over this morning? I assumed that must be your girlfriend because who else would make a funeral casserole for our family?"

"Sherry's my stepmom."

"Max remarried?"

He nodded. "About eight years ago now."

An awkward quiet hung between us. "I…"

My phone buzzed from my pocket. I pulled it out. It was a text from my mom asking where I was, telling me to come back to the hospital ASAP.

"Shit! Sorry. I gotta get back to my Grammy."

"Oh. Okay. Let's go."

Chapter Eight

Brad insisted on driving me to the hospital, which was probably for the best because I was shaken, and though it was a quick trip I wasn't sure if I would have been able to do it behind the wheel. When we got there, Mom and her new boytoy, Ernie, were in the waiting nook just outside the room. They were both sipping coffee. I didn't see GG anywhere.

"What's going on?" I asked my mom. "How's Grammy?"

She looked up at me and then at Brad. I swore she glared at him before she looked back down to her lap. "Luna," she began.

Her voice was not shaky, but it was somber. The pause after she said my name was so dramatically long, I wanted to scream at her to tell me what I already knew, but I didn't. I didn't want to hear it. I just didn't want to be in this space any longer.

"Your grandmother is now at peace," she finally managed to get out.

I saw Ernie take my mom's hand and give it a squeeze.

Brad's hand grazed mine, but I pulled away, turning and bolting. I had to get out there. And fast. I practically sprinted down the hallway past the ICU, past the gift shop and cafeteria, and didn't stop until I reached the Labor and Delivery ward. Turning in circles, I searched for the nursery, wondering if they still let you peek at the newborns from behind glass like they were exotic zoo creatures. It seemed like seeing tiny pink creatures right now might help distract me from my real emotions, the ones threatening to tighten around me and choke me.

Why I couldn't deal with them was beyond me. I had every right to be sad. The woman who raised and cared for me, the one person I could depend on throughout my life, who I spoke with weekly on the phone, who knew me better than anyone else, who I adored and loved more than any other, was gone. I had been in denial since she told me about the diagnosis only a month and a half ago. It was part of the reason I hadn't come back to see her. I had this weird idea that if I didn't believe she was dying, she wouldn't. I was so stupid and so very wrong.

I flung myself against the wall to keep from collapsing, and I breathed into my arms, trying to hold everything bottled in, even though I was depleted and tired of fighting it.

"Hey," I heard someone say.

I felt a light touch on my shoulder. "You okay?" Brad said.

"Yeah. I'm fine."

I turned to face him to, I don't know, prove that I was good. My grandmother was dead, but I hated the idea of letting people see that I was vulnerable. I tried so hard to not appear to have the same mental instabilities that I saw in my mother. I wanted to always come across as someone who was collected, mature, and normal—whatever that meant. Except Brad gave me a look, one I was so used to seeing during my youth, one that said he understood what I was going through. He had my back. So when he spread his arms open wide, before I could think, I buried myself deep inside his chest, and I let it all go.

"I'm so sorry," he said as he began to rub my back.

My tears flowed freely. It felt so right, but also so, so wrong. Why was I so conflicted and yet felt safer than I'd ever felt, safe enough to let myself cry in this person's arms? This person whom I thought of often over the last decade, but had not actually had any contact with. In many ways, he was a stranger to me. In that moment, I didn't care, I just went with it. After I got it all out, I broke away from him, wiping at my eyes and nose. "Can we get out of here?"

"Sure. Where do you want to go?"

"The beach."

He nodded.

****

The river was my happy place. From the time I could pedal, I would bomb my bike down the hills of Alton straight to the water as if the force of nature was so strong it pulled me right to it. It was my church, where I found something bigger. I spent hours sitting along the banks, collecting rocks, wading in, or walking the sandy shores. It was the closest thing this land-locked Midwest town had to an ocean. The water calmed and cleansed me, and when I'd started getting my panic attacks, I thought the river would be my answer, my cure. And while it did ease my anxiety, it did not stop the attacks. I'd read everything I could about anxiety and panic attacks over the years, but nothing led me to a conclusion about the cause of my own. All I knew was that I found solace from water, so I sought it out whenever I was feeling lost.

I hadn't spent a lot of time at the beach with Brad growing up because I preferred to go alone, but he was aware of how much it meant to me. If my mom had the red shed, I had the river as my mental sanctuary. But there was an occasion or two when we got old enough to drive when Brad would invite me along to a bonfire with friends of his from school. I had only gone a handful of times because I was always awkward in social situations, having little experience with parties and not knowing anybody else there besides Brad. Occasionally, Fia Butcher, my friend from second grade, would be there, and she and I would catch up briefly. Brad always went out of his way to introduce me to the other kids and make me feel welcome, but that was weird, too. And besides Fia, most of the other girls were standoffish or downright rude to me. I was sure they thought Brad and I were an item, so they immediately didn't like me.

We parked and walked over the dike and when I saw the water, I took a big gulp of air, feeling like I was reborn. "I've missed this place."

"The water's pretty high still," he said. "We had a lot of snow this winter."

He was right; there wasn't much beach, but there was enough to sit down, so we did. I tucked my knees up under me and looked out at the deep chasm of blue taking in the entire landscape, listening to the waves rolling in, feeling the light spring breeze on my face. It felt…like home.

We were quiet for a time, both locked in our own mental spaces. My emotions were all over the place, but as I ran through what had happened back there in the waiting area, I turned to Brad. "Did something happen between you and my mom while I was gone?"

"Happen? What do you mean?"

"I swore I thought she gave you a nasty look when

she saw you."

"That's not new. She'd been doing that since I started coming to the farm with my dad as a kid."

"Really? I never noticed it back then. Why would she not like you?"

He laughed. "I have no idea. I just assumed it was because I like you."

I nodded. "That's probably true." I paused. "It's terrible to say, but I'm angry that Grammy is gone and my mother is still here. I wish it was the other way around. I wish…Grammy had been my mom. Everything would have been so much…less complicated that way." I watched to see Brad's reaction to the purging of one of my deepest, ugliest thoughts.

He seemed unphased. "I get it. Sometimes I wonder how things might be different had I not lost my mom at such a young age, like if my dad had been killed in a car accident instead."

"And?" I asked him. "What's the answer? How do you think your life would have been different?"

"I dunno. I probably wouldn't have been close to you."

"Really? Why do you think that?"

"My dad wouldn't have dragged me kicking and screaming to the farm constantly."

"Ah. Right."

"And…I would probably be married by now, maybe have a kid or two."

"What's that got to do with your mom's death?"

It took him a long time to muster up the strength to say what was churning around in his brain. He looked down, picked up a small stone and rolled it around in his hand before tossing it out into the river. Keeping his eyes straight ahead where the rock had plunged in, he said, "I'm scared to fall in love. It's stupid, really. I just assume that the second I commit to someone, they're going to leave me, like it's me. I'm sure I'm the cause. My mom dying. Addy too. I wasn't close to my dad as a kid. I was a total mama's boy. And having her ripped away from me felt so personal. Like I was being punished. Like I'm cursed or something."

"You've never told me that before," I said.

He looked at me with total confusion plastered on his face. "When would I have told you that?"

"No. It's just…we used to talk about that kind of stuff when we were younger."

He shrugged and I sat quietly taking in the gravitas of what he'd confessed to me.

"Are you and your dad closer now?"

"In some ways, yes. I don't resent him, not like you do your mom, anyway."

I nodded. "Do you resent me?" I asked. "For not staying in touch?"

"Maybe a little," he admitted.

"Well, you could have reached out to me too, you know?"

"That's fair."

"So, you've never been in a relationship?" I asked him.

"I've dated some, but nothing serious." He paused. "What about you? Are you seeing anyone?"

"No."

"But I'm sure you have, right?"

"Not really."

"Why not?"

"Because of what I told you earlier, about the

attacks…because I'm…broken."

He laughed. "I'm cursed and you're broken. We make a great pair."

Chapter Nine

Brad took me back to the farm. It was well past noon and neither of us had eaten a thing yet. I asked if he wanted to come in and have some of the casserole his stepmom had made for us. He didn't have to be at the bar until four, and he was hungry, so he agreed.

As it was heating it up, we sat on the couch awkwardly. I pulled the old photo album from the bookshelf and brought it back to ease the weirdness. We paged through it sitting side-by-side. I hadn't looked through it in such a long time it was like I'd never seen it before. I figured Brad would get a kick out of it too, since our families had been so connected, and since he knew everyone from this town better than I did, he probably knew more people in the photos than me.

"Who's this?" Brad asked, pointing to one of the rare Andersen family photos.

"That's my Uncle Robbie. He died in a farming accident when he was pretty little."

In the picture, GG, Grammy, Mom, and Robbie were wearing their Sunday best. GG and Grammy were standing behind the kids. GG wasn't smiling because that was just how he rolled, but Grammy had a hand on each kid's shoulder, maybe to keep them in place, but she had a large grin on her face. She looked so happy and proud. It couldn't have been much later that the accident happened. I don't recall seeing any pictures of Robbie appearing much older than he was in this one.

"That's terrible. I didn't know that."

"Another one of those things that nobody in the family wants to talk about," I said. "I don't know much about it, except that he was apparently messing around on the combine when he wasn't supposed to be. It was parked in the old machine shed and he managed to start it up, but he was too little to control it. I don't know. I imagine he drove it into the wall and flipped it. It must have been bad."

"Yikes. That's awful."

"Yeah."

"I guess I can see why nobody wants to talk about that."

We turned the page of the album, ready to move on from that topic, and there was a small picture of me and Sonny sitting on a couch holding hands. It wasn't the plaid farm couch, so it had to have been in our apartment in Minneapolis. I'd probably looked at that picture a million times before, but now that I was older so many details stuck out to me that I hadn't seen before. The two of us didn't look at all like twins, even fraternal. Sonny had dark hair, dark eyes, and an olive complexion. I had lighter and paler features, blonde hair, and light green eyes. It was so strange that my mom named her for the sun and me for the moon, when it would have made more sense if they were switched based on our features.

But it was in the eyes, now that I was really examining the photo, that I realized where I'd seen them before.

"Does Sonny look like anyone familiar to you?" I asked Brad, pointing at the picture of my sister.

"I was just thinking how she doesn't look like you

at all," he said. "But familiar? I don't…"

"Your Uncle Mickey, maybe?"

He picked up the album and moved it closer to his face scrutinizing the photo. "Huh. You know…maybe a little. The darker hair and skin tone, though lots of people have those features. Why?"

"It's more than that. Look closer at the eyes. There's something really…I might be crazy, but your dad told me that Mickey and my mom dated back in the day, before he took off, so I'm wondering if Mickey is our…"

Before I finished telling Brad my theory, the back door near the kitchen opened and I turned to see Mom and GG come through it. I got up and went to GG, giving him a hug. He only tolerated it for a second before he asked what was in the oven.

"A hot dish that Max's wife made for us. It should be ready in a few minutes," I answered.

"Fine. I'm going to wash up then," he said.

After he climbed the stairs, I asked my mom how he was doing.

"He's a tough old geezer. He'll deal with it."

I nodded and traced my mom's eyes to Brad who still sat on the couch and then she said, "I'm going to rest. I'll eat later."

I sat back down on the couch next to Brad. Just as I did, the timer on the stove started buzzing, so I got up again to attend to it. I had no idea where Grammy kept the hot pads. I'd never really cooked in this kitchen. After opening every single drawer, I finally found them.

"Food is ready," I called, and set the glass baking dish on a hot pad on the butcher block counter. Then I took out the stack of plates and some silverware and set it down.

GG, Brad, and I sat down at the oak table with our plates. We ate in awkward silence. Brad kept his head practically glued to his plate, and GG was his usual stoic self, and even if he hadn't been, I wouldn't expect him to make small talk hours after losing his wife. I was frankly surprised to see him eating, but his take on food was that it was simply another chore that one got done and out of the way before moving on to the next chore.

I sat, pushing my food around on my plate trying to work out why my family members all seemed to dislike Brad. He told me there hadn't been any incidents while I was gone, in fact, he'd rarely been to the farm since I'd left or had much interaction with my family at all, so what else could it be? GG loved Max like a son, so by that logic, he should think of Brad like a grandchild, instead, he seemed to be giving him eyes of steel when he acknowledged his existence at all. It was odd because the only person I'd heard my grandfather really open up to, besides my grandma, was Max. The two of them could stand for hours talking their heads off, though it was almost always about farm work.

Between bites, GG looked up at me from across the table. "Where's the truck?"

"Oh, it, uh, broke down last night."

"Broke down? Where?"

"In the Finley's bar parking lot, but don't worry. I've already scheduled a tow truck to pick it up later tonight. Do you want me to have them bring it to Bowers Auto to check it out?"

GG grunted, thus ending the conversation.

Both Brad and GG powered through the food and got up to put their plates in the sink at virtually the same time. GG gave Brad a look and Brad backed away, waiting for a safe opening. "Thanks for the meal," he said. "I should be getting to work. Please let me know if there's anything I can do."

When GG didn't respond, I got up. "Do you want to take the dish back with you? I can put the rest of this in a different container."

He waved me off. "I can come and collect it later."

"Please thank Sherry for us," I said.

I walked Brad out to his car. "Sorry about GG."

"It's fine. He just lost his wife."

"Yeah." That was probably it, I thought to myself.

Brad kicked at some loose pebbles in the driveway. "You coming by the bar later?"

I nodded. "I gotta meet the tow truck driver."

"How'd you get home last night?"

"Your dad gave me a lift."

He looked back up at me. "My dad was at the bar?"

"No. He was driving by and saw GG's truck in the lot and thought it was odd, so he stopped."

"Oh. That makes more sense."

"Max doesn't frequent the bar?" I asked.

"Nope."

"Why?"

He shrugged. "It's not really his thing. This place, the land, your grandpa, that's where my dad's heart is. Always has been, always will be."

"You sound a little bitter about that," I said.

"I'm used to it." He pulled his phone out of his front pocket and checked the time. "Okay. I better run. See you later?"

I nodded and stood watching as Brad got into his car and backed down the long driveway. He gave a little wave at the end before taking off down the road. I felt like I was in a time warp, like he was just dropping me back home after we'd been hanging out. In some ways, it was comforting to know how easily we'd been able to pick right back up where we'd left off. In other ways, I felt like I was going in reverse. All of the strides I'd taken in getting away from this small town, this small life had brought me back around to being exactly where I was before I left. And yet, I had a weird teenage sensation stirring around inside of me that was familiar, too.

I wasn't sure if it was the fluttering of a crush or the thing I felt just before my attacks started to take hold. Could Brad have been right? Was he the cause of my attacks? Now that I knew he'd been there that first time while I was hidden away under the blanket, I realized he was there during other episodes too, like the time on the hill, and just a few nights ago at the bar. It made sense in that I hadn't had any attacks since leaving because Brad wasn't in New York.

It just didn't explain why he would cause me to have them. Could my anxiety honestly spike that much when I was around him? Why? I definitely cared about Brad, but I didn't think my feelings for him would make me crash that hard, unless…it wasn't love that was causing me to do it? Was there some other reason why I might subconsciously have an adverse reaction to the best friend I'd ever known? Clearly the rest of my family didn't seem too pleased by his presence. What was it about him? Was I missing something?

Chapter Ten

Back inside, I sat down to finish looking through the photos. GG had disappeared, likely back into the cow barn where his workshop was located. It was a small room off the back of the barn with a workbench and his tools. When I was little, he could spend all day tinkering with things there, and I imagined now that Grammy wasn't here to whistle for him to come back in, he'd likely never leave the confines of his shop again unless someone dragged him out by his hair and there wasn't much left to get a decent grip, so I worried about what was to come.

I looked at the photo album trying to distract myself from real problems. Re-examining the photo of Sonny, I suddenly remembered what I'd meant to tell Brad. I took my phone out and I did some searching online for the name Mickey Finley on all the major social media sites, but I didn't find anyone who looked like they might be around Mom's age. It didn't surprise me that much, because a man of that generation, much less one who had left town to get away from everyone, was probably not going to be inclined to put themselves out there, especially online. I didn't find anything of substance doing broad searches under the name either. I was at a dead end in more than one way.

Mom came back down the stairs. She was all dressed up in a floral skirt, a silk blouse, and heels. Her hair was curled and she had applied fresh makeup.

"I thought you were napping?"

"I did. Now Ernest is taking me out for a bite to eat. It's our date night."

Seemed like a strange way to grieve to me, but I didn't say it out loud.

"What are you planning to do?" she asked as she found her purse.

"I'm going to deal with the truck in an hour or so, and maybe I'll stop in and have a drink at the bar," I said, looking at her face for a reaction.

"I meant, what are you planning to do next?"

"Uh…"

"Oh, for Pete's sake, Luna. When are you going back to New York?"

"Well, I took two weeks off of work," I said.

"So you plan to stay another week?"

"Well, yeah. If not longer."

"Longer? Why?"

"If I didn't know better, I'd think you were trying to get rid of me."

She rolled her eyes. "I'm simply asking because I assumed you'd be on the next plane out of here the second you could."

"What about Grammy's service? And who will take care of GG now?"

My mom looked at the slim gold watch on her wrist. "I don't think we plan to have a service."

"What? Why not?"

"Grammy wanted to be cremated, and she said she'd rather us not make a fuss, for GG's sake. It's too hard for him. We'll spread her ashes in the orchard next to your sister."

"Oh."

"Does tomorrow morning work for you?"

"I…sure. Does GG know about this plan?"

She started toward the door. "I'm going to be late. Can you hunt him down and let him know, please?"

"Me?"

"Eight o'clock."

"You really want me to leave, don't you?"

She sighed. "I don't want you to feel like you need to stay, is all. And to answer your question, I can handle taking care of my own father. Who do you think has been doing it since you left?"

Grammy. That was who. I didn't say it out loud. My mother's hand was on the door handle. There wasn't enough time to start this argument now let alone finish it. "I'll see you tomorrow then, I guess," I said.

"Don't be late," my mother said as she slipped out the door in another all too familiar scene.

I wondered how many times I would experience déjà vu while I was here. My next thought was wondering how long I would be here because my mom was right. I would have loved more than anything to get out of here, but deep down I knew that was probably not going to happen, at least not anytime soon. How could I leave now? Not only did I not trust my mother to look after my grandfather, I also wasn't sure she could be trusted to be left to her own devices. Sure, she hadn't melted down since I'd been here, but it was only a matter of time.

After I heard her drive away, I got up and went in search of GG. I found him in the first place I searched. He was sitting in a chair he had set up near the hay shoot in the back of the loft. With the shoot open, there was a view of the back land, which consisted of Grammy's vegetable garden, which hadn't been planted this year, the big maple tree with the tire swing I'd spent many days under doodling in my notebook as a kid, and the pasture that led to the hill. It wasn't as nice a view as when one stood on the hill, but it was the Andersen property, GG's pride and joy. I didn't know everything about my grandfather, but I had figured out a few of his tricks by now. When things were tough, and he had some serious contemplating to do, he would head up to this spot. I believed it was where he talked to God. Now, I was guessing he was talking to Grammy. Nearly the same thing, in my opinion.

Seeing him there alone in that old chair practically tore my heart from my chest. I pulled the other chair over and sat beside him. It was a clear day. I surveyed the property as memories flooded in.

"You okay?" I asked him.

"About as good as I can be."

"Yeah. Me too."

GG sniffled and put his arm over my shoulder and gave it a squeeze.

"Mom wants to spread the ashes tomorrow morning. Are you up for that?"

"No, but it's what Gram wanted, so I'll do it."

"Good."

"Did you know my own granddaddy bought this land during the height of the Great Depression? He planted the first apple trees here. That whole side of the land had been orchard back in those days. When my daddy, August Andersen, took over, he bought the western portion of the land and planted the corn crops. 'Course, he rotated them out occasionally, but not wanting to be exactly like his father, he cut back the orchard and added the animals. I guess I didn't see any need to be different. I just wanted to keep a small portion of each of them here. My grands, Daddy, Mama, my brothers, and a baby sister too, Robert, Sonny, and now my sweet Ida. Generations of us resting under those apples."

"It's a nice spot. Grammy will be happy there."

He grunted.

****

Dealing with the tow truck in the parking lot took longer than I'd anticipated, and by the time GG's pickup was finally hoisted and ready to go off to the auto shop, I was drained and decided to head out instead of going inside the bar for a night cap. At least that was what I told myself. Deep down I think I may have been worried that I was going to have yet another panic attack if I went in. I knew it wasn't the alcohol causing the attacks because I went out with friends and colleagues for a drink now and again in New York without disastrous consequences, so what if Brad was right? What if he really was the trigger?

Thinking back to the times I'd experienced the episodes, I realized Brad had been around whether I'd remembered or not. But why would my best friend, my oldest confidante, cause me to experience some kind of bizarre mental breakdown when I was in his presence? It made no sense, yet I was scared it might be the truth.

I headed back to the hotel and decided not to think about it. Instead, I took a shower, ordered room service, put on a terrible cable movie, and had a good cry over the loss of my grandma. It had been a long, emotional day and I had to get up early to get back to the farm early the next day for what I assumed would be another emotionally taxing day, so I closed my eyes and tried to sleep.

Surprisingly, I woke up feeling rested, which I had not expected. It was unusual for me. Even at home in my own bed, I had wild bouts of insomnia. Sleep never came easily for me, and when it did finally come, I was often plagued by vague, nonsensical nightmares that never had meaning behind them except to cause me to wake suddenly in a full sweat feeling like the devil was close at hand. I chalked it up to being part and parcel of my anxiety. Though I'd been to therapy a few times and described these occurrences, nobody was ever able to figure out the culprit, and since night terrors can and do happen to lots of people for unknown reasons, and didn't really affect my day-to-day life, I didn't bother taking medication for it. Instead, I self-medicated with herbal supplements, or calming tea, or a drink before bed. I'd come to rely a little too heavily on the last one though and I'd been trying to ease up a bit. None of these things really seemed to help anyway. When the dreams wanted to come, they did. It was out of my control.

Regardless, I felt oddly refreshed this morning. I chalked it up to being incredibly exhausted. Whatever the case, I was in the rental car and on the way to the farm with plenty of time to spare, so I decided to stop for some coffee and a bouquet of flowers for Grammy. I was annoyed with my mother for telling me not to be late, anyway. She was the one who was consistently late for things, not me.

I pulled into Crane's Drug at quarter to eight and noticed the sign taped to the door. *Back in 15 minutes. Sorry for the inconvenience.* This sort of thing only happened in small towns. It was a pharmacy for crying out loud. Did they not have more than one person working? I had no way of knowing if the sign had been taped to the door fourteen minutes before I arrived or one minute. I looked at the time on my phone. I was only five minutes from the farm. What did it matter if I was a few minutes late anyway? It wasn't like this was a formal ceremony. It was just going to be the family.

I got back into the rental car and checked emails on my phone while I waited for someone to return to the store. I decided I'd give them five minutes, and if they still weren't back, I'd forgo the coffee and flowers. But after waiting nearly eight minutes, I realized I was in too deep to just leave now. After ten minutes, I glanced up and saw a line forming at the door. Shortly thereafter, someone opened the door and people began to shuffle inside. I got out of the car and sprinted in to make my purchase.

Once I had my items, there was another short wait to check out. No self-checkout in a tiny drug store that still looked like the 1980s had exploded inside of it. As I stood in line, the woman in front of me turned around. She was roughly my mother's age. "Are you Jenny Andersen's daughter, by chance?"

"I am," I said.

"Thought so. Haven't seen you around in a long time."

"No. I'm only back for a short visit."

She kept looking at me, as if she was waiting for me to ask her something, so I said, "Are you friends with my mom?"

"Me?" She shook her head and laughed in a few short bursts. "No."

She turned back to face the check-out counter again as if nothing had ever been said. This was the reason why I hated Alton. I checked the time again wishing I'd skipped the flowers altogether. But she stepped up to the counter and I was next.

****

When I pulled onto the property, it was twelve minutes past eight. I was hoping to not see my mother's car in front of the garage, but it was there along with two other cars. I recognized Max's car, but not the other one. I jumped out and met my mother coming toward me.

"I thought I said don't be late," was the first thing out of her mouth.

"I'm only ten minutes late and it wasn't my fault…"

"Come on," she said, walking past me headed toward the orchard. "Everyone's waiting."

"Who is everyone?" I said, with the flowers in one hand and coffee in my other.

She didn't bother to answer. Soon enough, I saw. Max, GG, Ernie, and another man I did not recognize, but who was dressed very formally, all stood hovering around the tree that we'd scattered Sonny's ashes under all those years ago. I wanted to ask who the stranger was, but I didn't get a chance because the moment I got close enough, my mother looked at him and told him to go ahead and start, and he began speaking.

"We are gathered here on this lovely spring day to celebrate the life of a lovely woman: Ida Dee Andersen."

Apparently, he was officiating the memorial, which was interesting. He must have been from the little white church at the bottom of the hill that Grammy attended. I couldn't for the life of me remember the name of the church because Grammy always called it the little white church. I knew she went to church, but she'd often done it alone. GG, while he may have believed in a higher power, did not attend Sunday services. This land was his religion. My mother had flat out refused to go, as far as I could recall. I had gone along with Grammy from time to time growing up, but I wasn't required to go and there were many times when I would come downstairs on a Sunday morning and she was already gone. I was pretty sure she preferred going by herself. It was a personal thing for her—religion. She didn't go every Sunday, only when she felt the need. I could respect that as it was the same way I thought about church. I wasn't opposed, but I didn't have to go regularly. And because I hadn't gone much, I had no idea what the position of this religious person was. Was he the pastor? Another clergy-type person? Or did he simply officiate funerals?

Whatever his position, the church man was handsome and younger than I'd expect from a man of the cloth, if that was even what he was. Was I even allowed to think such things of him? Probably not and especially not at my grandmother's funeral, which wasn't supposed to be a funeral in the first place. Or maybe it was and I just wasn't told. I could blame my mother for this, I was sure on that point.

I tried to stop fixating on him and instead focus on Grammy. He went on to say a few more pleasantries about my grandmother, which were true but not very personal in nature. Had he known her? Given her irregular attendance at the little white church at the bottom of the hill, I'd say he did not know her, or at least very well. It wasn't his fault. It was still more than I expected to hear being spoken about her today. I assumed we wouldn't say anything at all, as was the custom of my family. I expected GG to tip the urn, spill out the ashes, and then pivot on his work boots and head right back to the barn while the rest of us stood silently with our own thoughts before we also turned and headed back to where we'd once come from.

Instead, after the stranger from the church spoke, Mom cleared her throat. "I wrote a poem I'd like to share," she said.

A poem? I clutched my coffee tightly as she began to read from a small piece of lined notebook paper she pulled from her pants' pocket.

A new planting season has begun.

A tiny insect climbs through the dirt.

Working her way through the mounds of freshly churned soil,

Pushing outward.

Higher, higher.

Until she reaches the final plateau.

Beyond the dangers lurking.

From the machines and predators.

Safe now.

She spreads her wings and flies.

To greener pastures.

By the time she finished, I was sobbing. I tried to be discreet, but I struggled with my full hands to finagle a tissue from my purse so I could wipe my eyes. I ended up setting my coffee down on the ground, but held onto the flowers. When I found my tissue, I dabbed at my eyes. That my mother's words could move me in such a way was something new and surprising to me. I couldn't compete with what she'd written, nor did I want to try. I hadn't prepared anything to say, so I was glad I'd stopped for the flowers after all.

When I looked up everyone was staring at me, so I staggered forward feeling all of the eyes upon me. I set the spring bouquet down against the apple tree and said, "Love you, Grammy," before stepping back to my place.

When the ashes were spread, by the church man and not GG this time, we all turned and dispersed in different directions. Max went toward the pole barn, GG to the cows. Mom and Ernie held hands while walking back to their car, and I followed behind them with the man from the church.

"You're from the little white church at the bottom of the hill, right? The one my grandmother attended?" I asked him.

"The church of St. Joseph. That's right," he said. "You're Ida's granddaughter, aren't you?"

I nodded. "I'm Luna."

"Daniel. Very nice to meet you. She talked about you often. She was extremely proud of you. The granddaughter who was making it in the Big Apple. That's what she always told people."

A warmth spread through me. "Really? I didn't know that."

"What do you do in the Big Apple, if I may ask?"

"I work in advertising."

He nodded. I had no idea what else to say, so per usual, I put my foot in my mouth. "Thank God it wasn't a windy day."

He gave me a side eye.

"For spreading the ashes. You know? So they didn't blow back?"

"Oh, right."

"Anyway, thank you for coming today," I said. "It was a nice service."

We reached his car. By this point, I was ready to just hightail it out of there, but Daniel stopped and turned to me. "If you ever feel like talking, just come down the hill. The doors are always open."

"Oh. Okay. Thanks. I might."

After I watched him drive away, I contemplated the invitation, then I pivoted and headed up to the hill and sat on a stump for a good long while.

Chapter Eleven

The next morning, I checked my phone and saw I had a text message from my mom asking to meet her and Ernie for breakfast. I agreed, but not without extreme trepidation. I couldn't put my finger on why I had a bad feeling about it, but it wasn't like my mother to invite me to do anything with her out of the goodness of her heart. She didn't operate like that. So, I drove over to the restaurant trying to work out what her angle might be.

The restaurant was one Grammy and GG had taken me to as a kid quite a few times. The Alton Inn was the only fancy sit-down place to eat in town. It had once been a turn-of-the-century saloon that catered to people who'd worked on the river during the lumber era with an inn above it. A big two-story, colonial-style building, it was built right on the waterfront. It didn't have a saloon vibe anymore, more like a senior citizen eatery, but I loved thinking about the history of it.

While it had been renovated many times over, it hadn't been updated much in the last few decades. It was exactly how I remembered it as a kid, right down to the art on the wall and the aroma of flowers and bacon that filled the restaurant. It was like a funeral was taking place inside of a diner. That was what I imagined the scent to be.

I made absolutely certain to be on time this morning, but looking around the dining area, I didn't see Mom and

Ernie anywhere. The hostess seated me at a table looking out toward the water, which I appreciated. I calmed my nerves with coffee while staring out at the river as I waited for whatever bomb was about to be dropped on me. I knew there had to be one, I just wasn't sure what it could be. Something regarding GG maybe? We still hadn't fully discussed what our plan would be when I headed back yet with regards to GG's care.

While I knew he was physically capable and still sound of mind, I worried about him because Grammy had done so much of the housework, including the finances and all of the cooking and cleaning. A thought popped into my head that Mom might be considering selling the farm. In some ways, it made sense, though I didn't think GG would ever agree to that.

I checked the time. They were late. Retribution for my tardiness from the day before, no doubt. As the clock ticked, my anxiety levels climbed. Even the water wasn't able to keep my wild thoughts in check. Surprisingly, I never once felt as though I was about to have a panic attack. It was weird how they worked. They were so unpredictable that they never reared up during times when it seemed most logical for them to do so. It was often the opposite, really. They came on when I was least expecting them. Nevertheless, I drank my coffee and grew more and more tense with each minute I waited.

When they finally arrived, I was more angry than I was nervous. They, on the other hand, seemed to be in good spirits, giddy even. "Morning, Luna," my mother said, as she sat down across from me at the table.

"You're twenty-five minutes late," I said.

"Sorry about that," Ernie said, sitting down. "I take full responsibility. I was on a call. Car accident. It always seems to happen when you have reservations. Murphy's law, I guess."

"Oh," I said. "Was…everyone okay?"

"Yeah. Just a fender bender, really."

"That's good."

When they walked in, I noticed for the first time how oddly paired they looked side-by-side. My mother being tall and slender, wearing black pants with a lacy cardigan over a white top. Ernie, I realized, was squat and overall small in stature, but since he was also wearing a short-sleeved polo shirt and khakis, in contrast to his smallness, he had a pair of bulging biceps peeking out of his sleeves which surprised me. It didn't go with his glasses and lack of hair. He was like business on top and macho-man in the middle. I had no idea what the bottom half of him was like and I was perfectly okay with that.

The server brought menus and we ordered drinks and started looking at the menus, so it wasn't until the drinks actually arrived and my mother picked up her glass that I noticed a shiny piece of jewelry on her left ring finger. A gold band with a large diamond setting. Her eyes watched me as I processed the information.

"Mom? What's that ring? Are you…"

She smirked and held out her hand to me. "That's what we wanted to tell you. Ernie proposed to me. We're getting married!"

The reaction I was meant to have was the exact opposite of the one I did have. I tried very hard to not let my face show what my insides were feeling, but I wasn't good at hiding internal strife. My default was to ask questions. "Um, what?"

"I believe congratulations is the word you're looking for, Luna," she said, sternly.

I shook my head quickly trying to recalibrate. "No. I…just wasn't expecting this. I mean…how long have you even known one another for?"

Ernie chimed in. "Listen, I know you have concerns, but your mother and I have been together long enough to know that this is what we both want." He reached over and squeezed her hand. She smiled at him before they leaned into one another and kissed. I, on the other hand, tried not to vomit.

"Okay, but…"

"Luna," my mother snapped. "Please don't be rude. Ernie insisted on inviting you to breakfast to tell you the good news in person. Remember your manners. I taught you better…"

I wanted nothing more than to stand up and tell her that she didn't teach me anything except how to run when things got too hard, but I couldn't do that now because we were in public and didn't want to make a scene. Plus, I glanced over at Ernie who sat looking at me with a big, dumb grin on his face. So I gritted my teeth and said it. "Congratulations."

"Thank you," she replied smugly.

My mother quickly changed the subject knowing we were walking on fragile ground and we discussed safer topics like the weather until the food arrived. But I couldn't help but come back to it, so after I poured syrup on my pancakes, I said, "Do you have a date in mind yet? For the wedding?"

They exchanged a look and then Ernie said, "We'd like to have it at the end of June."

"Next June, right?"

"No," my mother said. "This summer."

I nearly choked on my pancakes. "It's already the

end of May. Don't you need more time to schedule the caterer and all of that?"

"It will be small," she said. "We're going to do it on the farm. Nothing fancy."

"We'd love for you to be there," Ernie added. He patted my hand gently and then squeezed it. I smiled at him, but it wasn't easy because my head swirled with questions, things that needed sorting. "Then what?" I asked. "Where will you live?"

More looks were exchanged between them before my mother said, "We'll live at Ernie's home, down in the valley."

"What about GG? Who will look after him?"

"He'll be fine," she said.

I somehow knew that would be her answer. She could only think about herself and what she wanted. I was about to argue with her, but I saw someone who had been seated a few tables over get up and start walking toward our table.

A woman in her sixties, dressed to the nines, stopped in front of my mother. "Jennifer, so good to see you. I don't mean to intrude, just wanted to say hello."

My mother stood and they hugged. "Marilynn, I haven't seen you in ages."

"I've been meaning to come by the gallery. I just haven't had much time lately. Is that fabulous piece I had my eye on still for sale?"

"It's not, but I'm sure we can find you something else. Lots of great new work has come in recently."

"Well, shoot. I really had my heart set on that one."

"Stop by sometime and see our newest collection."

"I will."

"Okay. You take care, Marilynn."

My mother sat back down and took a sip of her mimosa like nothing out of the ordinary had just taken place.

I stared at her, my eyes boring into her skull, but she nonchalantly picked up her fork and started back on her hashbrowns. "Mom? Who was that?"

"Oh, Marilynn is a client of mine."

"A client?"

"From the art gallery in Saltwater."

"Huh?"

"The place where I work."

"You work at an art gallery in Saltwater?"

She nodded.

"Since when?"

"Since a couple of years ago."

"Why, for the love of God, has nobody told me this?"

My mom simply gave me a blank look. "I guess you never asked."

When the bill came, Ernie insisted on paying. And when I stood up to leave, my mother didn't bother getting up, but Ernie stood and said, "Can I hug you?"

"Oh…okay."

As he wrapped his bulging biceps around me, he said, "I'm so happy to have a daughter. I would love it if you called me Dad."

I was so taken aback I almost pushed him away, but instead, we broke apart and I pivoted and fled the restaurant as fast as humanly possible.

Chapter Twelve

Being only steps from the river, it was a no-brainer to simply walk north along the shoreline to my spot. The day was cool and breezy like most spring days in Minnesota. I didn't care. I just needed to be alone with the water and my thoughts. The whole marriage thing was enough to pull me straight over the edge, but I couldn't shake Ernie's comment calling him dad. That was the last thing I wanted to call him.

The whole thing felt like a complete and total disaster, and the one person I wanted to talk to about it, the person who would truly understand what I was going through, wasn't here anymore. My grandma was my best friend, my sounding board, my moral compass. She knew how trying my mother was. She understood. It might seem weird to have an eighty year old as a bestie, but lots of adult women were close to their mothers. She had been a mother to me. I felt so desperately alone.

When I got to the public beach, the same spot where Brad and I had come a few days before, I plopped down and let the depth of my despair settle around me. I tucked my head into my lap and listened to the water, wishing things were different. I came up for air after a time and looked out toward the water again, watching the whitecaps churning in the wind, understanding the chaos of the scene. A few seagulls squawked and flew overhead toward something causing a commotion behind me. I turned to look.

"Hey," Brad said, walking my way. "I thought I might find you here this morning."

He sat down next to me.

"What are you doing here?"

"I was worried about you. You said you were going to stop into the bar."

"Right. Sorry. I was too worn out."

"I get it," he said. "Are you okay?"

"No. Not really." I wiped a tear away. "My mother just told me that she's getting married. And Ernie said I could call him Dad."

"Oh, yikes."

"Yeah."

"I'm so sorry."

"I don't know what to do. I feel like I need to somehow put a stop to it, but she's a grown adult. And if it does happen, there won't be anybody at the farm to keep an eye on GG."

"I'm sure my dad would be happy to do that."

"I can't ask him to do that. He's got too many other responsibilities. Besides, it's stuff like cooking and cleaning."

"You could hire someone," Brad offered.

"I guess so."

"It will all work out."

I turned to look at him. "You're probably right. I was overreacting. Thanks. I feel a lot better."

He smiled. "Good. Though I kinda wish I'd have kept my mouth shut."

"What do you mean?"

"Well, for a second there, it sounded a little like you were thinking about staying. I was hoping maybe, just maybe, my curse was finally broken."

Before I knew what was happening, Brad was leaning into me, and my immediate, no thought response was to meet him halfway, but then I hesitated and pulled back. "Brad, I—"

"Another panic attack?"

"No."

"I get it," he said, the familiar dejected look from our teen years plastered all over his face. "I thought since you asked me why I hadn't tried kissing you again, you were interested, but I guess you're still allergic to me."

"No! It's not that. It's…do you remember how we were talking in the living room when we were looking at the photo album?"

"Yeah."

"I'd started telling you something before GG interrupted. It's been weighing on me."

"What? That whole thing about how your sister maybe looked a little like…"

"Your uncle. Do you see where I'm going with this? Did you catch the part where I said that your dad told me that Mickey and my mom dated just before he took off and my mom went to college? Shortly after that, she was pregnant."

"Uh…"

"Yeah. So, if your uncle is my dad…"

"We might be cousins," he said.

I nodded. "Yep."

"Holy shit."

"Yep."

We both took a second to let the weight of it sink in. I had been mulling it around since the first night I saw the picture of Mickey in the bar, but I hadn't really given myself time to believe it. Part of me hoped to come up with something to counter it. Another part of me wanted it to be true because that would mean I would finally know who my dad was. Saying it out loud made the possibility of it get really real.

"But, we don't know if it's true," he said, with some mild hope threaded into his voice.

"We don't know if it's not true either," I added.

"Wow." He blew air out of his lungs and ran his hands through his shaggy hair. "But, like I was saying in your living room, you don't resemble Uncle Mickey at all. I don't think it's possible."

"Sonny and I weren't identical twins. We were fraternal. I could have taken on more of the Andersen traits and she could have had more of the Finley's side."

"Jesus," Brad muttered into the sand. "K. How are we gonna find out for sure?"

"I don't know."

"You need to go to your mom and demand she tells you," he said.

"I tried that the first day I arrived. Hell, I've been trying that since I was twelve. It's not the answer. She won't say, for whatever reason. I tried to do some online sleuthing, but I wasn't able to find a single thing about Mickey on the Internet."

"That makes sense. The guy is obviously not wanting to be found. I wouldn't expect him to have a social media account."

"Maybe you can do some detective work. Talk to Kelsey and your dad again. See if anybody knows anything that might lead us to Mickey's current whereabouts. Someone in the family has to know where he is."

"Okay. Yeah. I will. What are we gonna do if we locate him?"

"Go and talk to him, I guess. Hope he has answers."

"And if we can't? Or he doesn't?"

"I dunno. I guess we could take a DNA test."

"God. This is starting to sound like a bad daytime talk show," Brad said.

"It is. It really is."

****

After Brad left, I took a few more minutes looking out at the water, breathing deeply. So much noise swam around in my brain and I was absolutely certain nothing would quiet it until we learned something more about Mickey. The one good thing was that for the first time in twenty some years, I may have had a possible lead. Would my anxiety subside if and when I knew for sure who my father was? I believed it would.

I got up and instead of walking back the way I'd come trudging through the sand to return to my car in the Alton Inn parking lot, I decided to take the streets that ran through the neighborhood.

I hadn't been this way since I was a kid. It was funny how back then the houses were just regular, old homes in my tiny mind. I hadn't speculated much beyond that. Now, I realized how incredibly minute most of them were. Usually, huge estates were built along waterfront property, but not in Alton. Here the houses were leftovers from the last century when wealthy families from the cities had vacation properties built here en masse. They were hardly bigger than postage stamps as they were intended for weekend use, but many of them still existed. This was a working class neighborhood, so these affordable homes suited people around here just fine. Where else could you get a place with a water view for under six figures? Probably nowhere these days.

As I took a literal stroll down memory lane, I turned onto Autumn Avenue and recognized several homes as those belonging to early childhood friends from my elementary school days. One in particular stood out to me. A small forest green house with a brown fence that belonged to my best friend from kindergarten to third grade. Fia Butcher and I had remained in touch to some extent throughout the rest of our school days, having occasional sleepovers and attending each other's birthday parties. It wasn't a deep connection, not anything like Brad and I shared, but we did have some shared similarities that bonded us to an extent. We were both fairly reserved, lacking in the friend department, and neither of us had a dad.

She and I emailed a few times after I moved to New York, and we friended one another on social media, but it had been a long time since I'd heard anything from her or seen any updates to her online accounts. I wasn't even sure if she still lived in Alton.

Her house looked more or less the same as it had when I was a kid. There were several children's bicycles lying in a cluster near the driveway. Fia's mom, Diana, ran a daycare back in the day. She was the exact opposite of my own mother. She was boisterous and affectionate. She was one of those ladies who would take in stray kids like some took in stray animals. While Fia and a few others were her biological children, she also had foster children that would rotate in and out of the hoard of daycare kids. The house seemed to always be wild with excitement, which was also very different from my own, so I enjoyed being there.

Just as I made my way past the driveway, Diana came out the front door. She had aged quite a bit in the time I was away. Her hair was in a long, gray braid and she'd put on some weight. I imagine taking care of all of those kids would do that to a person.

I froze and waited as she made her way toward the middle of her driveway and then I walked toward her. "Diana? Hi! You probably don't remember me, but—"

She squinted at me and then said, "Luna Andersen? Is that you?" Before I could even answer she had wrapped me in a massive bear hug. She pulled back and looked at me. "How are you? I heard you were in New York and working in publishing."

I nodded. "Technically, it's advertising and illustration, but yeah."

"That's great! Good for you."

"Thanks. How's Fia? Is she still in Alton?"

"She lives in Marina now, but she works at the Alton Clinic as a GP. She's a doctor, you know."

"Oh! Wow. I didn't know that. Though it doesn't surprise me."

"She always was smart as a whip," Diana said with a proud beam. "You should give her a call while you're here. I'm sure she would love to see you. Come on in. I'll jot her number down for you."

"Okay. Thanks."

I followed Diana inside. The interior of the house looked almost the same as I remembered it. She grabbed a small notepad and pen and wrote down a phone number. "Her last name isn't Butcher anymore. It's Huller. She's married now." Diana ripped out the page and handed it to me. "That reminds me. I heard your mom and Ernie Schmitt are finally making it official."

My face must have distorted in a way that Diana couldn't make heads or tails of because she said, "Word travels fast in the valley."

"Right. But what did you mean when you said finally?"

She chuckled. "Oh, they went to senior prom together."

"Are you sure? I thought she was dating Mickey Finley."

"Hmm. I don't know about that, but I am sure about this, because I was a freshman at the time and I was friends with Ernie's younger sister, Bethany, and I thought he was pretty cool back then. Actually, you kinda remind me of Bethany. What year were you born again?"

"1990."

"Mmmm." She took a longer look at me. "And that prom would have been in 1989, right?"

I had no words. I shoved the phone number into my pocket. "Thanks for the number. It was great to see you again," I fumbled for the door and sprinted past the pile of bikes and down the driveway like I'd just seen a ghost. I felt dizzy, but not because a panic attack was on the horizon but because this new information changed everything.

When I got to my car, I was panting. I got in and drove as I sorted what I knew. It made sense. If Ernie and my mom had gone to prom together, it may have been the reason Mickey took off. He was likely angry and jealous that she'd gone to the dance with someone else. And it also meant that when Ernie said I could call him dad, maybe it was because he actually was my dad.

Chapter Thirteen

I packed up my things under a cloudy haze, and checked out of the hotel, deciding to stay with GG at the farm until I headed back to New York. There was no longer a need to be near the hospital and I wanted to make sure GG was going to be okay before I left.

When I got there, he was nowhere to be found, so I used the hidden key again and let myself inside. I put my bags down in my old bedroom and I started making him some dinner.

While I spread butter on GG's bread, I continued to think about Ernie and the possibility of him being my biological father. For some reason, it wasn't sitting well with me and I couldn't figure out why. Wasn't this the thing I'd wanted, been craving for so long? And if it was him, it would mean that Brad and I weren't first cousins. These were all good things. So, what was wrong? Why did I feel like it was not right? Ernie was okay. He was fine. I should have been happy about this possible revelation, instead, I was thinking of ways to discount it. Why? I suppose it was because he wasn't the superhero I'd formed in my head. Not only that, but he was on Mom's side. He wasn't going to save me from her. He was…going to marry her.

The one thing that still made no sense to me was that if Ernie was my dad, why would that have been kept such a guarded secret? Especially now. He seemed more than enthusiastic about me calling him dad. The only explanation was that my mother hadn't informed him of her situation back then or perhaps she had been with both Mickey and Ernie and didn't know who had actually fathered us.

When I finished making the food, I went out on the property in search of GG. This time, I found him pretty quickly in his workshop. He and I headed back in and sat down at the table. "Have you heard the news about Mom and Ernie?" I asked him.

He nodded. It hadn't surprised me that I was the last to be informed.

"And you're okay with it?"

GG bit into his ham. "You remembered the butter. It's good."

I smiled and waited for his reply to my question. He chewed on it and then ham and then he finally said, "He'll take good care of Jenny. That much I know. Can't know anything beyond that. Besides, she's an adult. What else can we do?"

This time, I nodded. "I checked out of the hotel. Can I stay here for a few nights?"

"This is your home," he said. "You're always welcome here."

"I have to go back to work soon."

"I figured."

"Will you be okay here alone?"

"Gonna have to be," he said.

"We could hire someone to come and do some cleaning and cooking a few times a week."

He waved the idea off. "Pffft."

"I'd feel better if you had someone coming to check up on you once and a while."

"Max will be around and I'm sure Jenny will come by now and again."

"Okay."

I finally gave in, making a mental note to have a discussion with Max before I left knowing I couldn't trust my mother to be responsible enough to be left in charge. I wasn't even sure if she knew how to cook. I'd never seen her or GG step foot behind Grammy's butcher block counter beyond just setting their dishes in the sink or getting a glass of water. Maybe things had changed since I'd left, but if I knew Grammy, I highly doubted it.

She probably was still cooking and cleaning well into the depth of her illness. I bet they had to drag her out of here kicking and hollering. Mom had told me that she wouldn't let them take her to the hospital until things had gotten so bad, she didn't have much choice. Which was why by the time I was called and finally got to the hospital, it was so quick. She was a tough, resilient lady. My mother did not inherit those traits from her.

"GG? Did you know that Mom and Ernie went to prom together?"

He raised his brow slightly. "Is that so?"

"According to Diana Butcher. I ran into her in town. Do you think there's a photo or two in one of the albums of Mom and her prom date?" I jumped up to take a look at the reference shelf, annoyed that I hadn't thought to check earlier.

"Could be, though Jenny was a wild child. It was always hard to wrangle her. Yer Gram was better at it than me, but even she picked her battles. Sometimes we didn't bother trying because she often pushed back. If I recall now," he said, scratching his stocking cap, "We were pleased because she was gonna go to the dance with a different fella than that one she'd been seeing. We didn't care for him and we told her as much. I remember Ida had asked her to bring her date around before the dance for a picture, but it didn't happen. I think she rode off on the back of a motorcycle before we even got eyes on the fella."

I brought the albums back to the table and set them in front of me. "Motorcycle? Did Ernie ride a motorcycle?" He did not seem the type, though I knew Mickey was exactly the type.

"Like I said, didn't get a good look at him. They were gone in a flash."

"GG? Do you think...Ernie could be my dad?"

"Can't say he isn't, but I can't say he is either. I suppose it's possible. There's something familiar about him, I'll say that much. Don't know for sure. If I did, I'd tell ya." He paused. "You could do a lot worse than Ernie for a dad."

"I know," I said, still not willing to accept it. "But...if Ernie's my dad, then...why do you and Mom dislike Brad so much?"

GG looked puzzled. "Huh? What do the two have to do with one another?"

"I dunno. Nothing." I shook my head. "Forget it." I felt stupid thinking Mickey may have been my father now. I figured that was the reason everyone was treating Brad poorly, because if they knew we were cousins, that would be a reason to try to keep us apart if they thought there might be some romantic feelings happening. But GG said he didn't know who my father was for sure and I trusted him. He wouldn't lie to me. Grammy had always told me the same thing. Over and over again. "I would tell ya, honey, if I knew."

I started flipping through the albums hoping they would offer up their secrets. Grammy hadn't put the pictures in chronological order, so I had to flip through each one of the yellowing pages with the crinkly, clear film glued over the top hunting frantically for clues.

GG had lost interest, finished his sandwich, and left by the time I had looked through all of the pages of the albums. He'd been right. There were no pictures of my mother in an apparent prom dress, and though I searched intently, I found no one resembling a younger version of Ernie hidden posing among the dated versions of friends and family either. I realized that I wasn't looking for proof any longer that Ernie was my dad, but rather, I was looking for evidence to discredit the possibility.

My phone buzzed. Brad and I had exchanged numbers before parting at the beach in case either of us figured anything out. He asked if I wanted to come by the bar later. I agreed, but I was also hesitant, because I'd made a decision that I wasn't looking forward to telling him.

Chapter Fourteen

It hadn't occurred to me that it was Friday night until I turned into the bar parking lot and saw all of the cars. Friday nights were notoriously busy bar nights in a small town because it was payday. For the first time since my arrival almost a week ago, the place was packed. I had to stand at the bar for a while and wait for someone to leave before I could sit down. There were even two bartenders on duty, splitting the bar in half. Even if I had been able to get a seat on the side of the bar Brad was tending, it was too busy for us to have done much chatting, not to mention, the noise echoed off the walls of the small space making it hard to hear much.

As last call approached, I'd had one too many. I wasn't a big drinker, and it didn't help that I had all but forgotten to eat with GG because I was too busy flipping through the photo albums on another wild goose chase that didn't pan out. I was bummed about it and I was also nervous to talk to Brad.

I thought I had been sipping my drinks slowly enough as I waited for things to die down, so I could tell him the thing that was on my mind, the thing I didn't expect him to take very well, but the alcohol hit me hard all of a sudden. I switched to water, but it was too late. I was too tipsy to drive, so I waited for Brad to close the place up so he could take me home. He suggested we go to his place for a late dinner and maybe a coffee first. I agreed because I still needed to talk to him. And I was curious to see how adult Brad lived.

When we turned into the driveway, I laughed.

"What?" he said.

"This is your house, silly."

"I know. I thought I was making us dinner?"

"I mean, this is the house you grew up in."

"Yeah."

"Did you forget we're not teenagers anymore?"

"I still live here," he said.

I laughed again. "You still live with your dad?"

"No," he said, pulling into the attached garage. "He moved in with Sherry when they got married, so I kept this place."

"Oh." I covered my mouth trying to stifle more laughter. "Is it weird? To still live in your childhood home?"

He shrugged. "Not really. Doesn't bother me."

We sat in the car in the garage for a minute while the door closed behind us.

"Sorry," I said. "It's not you. I laugh a lot when I've had too much."

He smiled.

"Did you ever bring a girl home? When we were younger?"

"Uh…"

I shoved him, probably a little too hard. "You did!"

"Maybe," he admitted with an embarrassed smirk.

"Who was she?"

"Nobody you knew. And…it was after you left."

"Oh. Okay."

"Why? Are you jealous?" he asked.

I thought about it for a second. "Maybe." Then I

leaned into him and tried to kiss him.

He pulled back. "Whoa, there."

"What's wrong?" I said.

"Come on," he said. "Let's get you some coffee."

I had been inside the house several times growing up. Oftentimes I would be running errands with GG and he needed to stop to see Max about something or other. We had also attended many bar-be-ques and family parties at this house, and during those occasions, the kids always roamed free. It wasn't a giant house, but I remember it had a cozy quality to it and I had fond memories of being here. As Brad opened the garage door, I wondered if it was going to be like the farmhouse—unchanged by time.

Brad led me inside the kitchen and I was shocked. It looked nothing like I remembered. In fact, it was very modern, even more modern than my taste. "Wow," I said. "I love what you've done with the place."

"Yeah? You like it? I had the whole thing redone a few years ago."

"I do. Not at all what I was expecting, but it's very nice."

"What were you expecting?" he asked.

"I was expecting it to feel like a bachelor pad. You know…like sports themed or something."

He furrowed his brow. "Sports themed?"

"I don't know!" I said with another laugh. "I'm drunk!"

"I'll say. Have a seat and I'll whip us up something."

I sat down at another bar stool, this one at Brad's marble kitchen island. I almost laughed again, but managed to hold it in.

He opened the fridge. "What are you hungry for?"

"Whatever you have. I feel bad having you wait on me after you were on your feet waiting on people all night."

"Eh, I'm used to it," he said, pulling some things out. "How about burgers?"

"Sounds perfect."

He got a pot of coffee brewing and started to form the hamburger patties. When the coffee was brewed, he poured me a cup and said, "So, I talked to Kelsey earlier. She said she had heard that Mick was driving trucks for a living, so he moved around a lot. The last place she knew he'd been living was in Davenport, Iowa. She said that was several years ago now though. I checked online and didn't find him in any current listings in Iowa."

I wasn't sure if it was the coffee or the conversation, but I was suddenly sober. "Oh, God" I said. "I just realized that…Oh, shit. Brad…"

"What?"

"None of that matters anymore," I said.

He raised his brow. "Why not?"

"I forgot to tell you…" I explained the whole deal with Ernie while he grilled the burgers. When I was done, he turned toward me. "Ernie Schmitt? Your biological dad? Huh. I'm not sure."

"Why not? It all adds up."

"Except the part about Gus telling you she got on the back of a motorcycle and sped off. That sounds more like Mickey than Ernie to me."

"But she was in the homecoming ceremony with Ernie, so how she got there and who she ended up with might be the reason Mickey bowed out. And then at some point during her freshman year of college, Sonny and I were born. And Diana said I look like Ernie's sister."

"Bethany? Wait. I know Beth. She comes into the bar every now and again. Trust me, you do not look a thing like Bethany Schmitt."

"Maybe not now," I said. "She was referring to her when she was younger."

Brad shook his head. "Hmmm."

I took a deep breath before I said the next thing—the thing I'd been chewing on all afternoon. "Anyway, I booked a ticket home. I'm leaving the day after tomorrow."

Brad's expression changed. "Without finding out for sure?"

"I don't think I'll ever know for sure."

"We just started digging."

"I'm done," I said. "I don't want to dig anymore."

"Why not?"

I shrugged. "I dunno. It's too hard. I keep having attacks and I…"

"Just want to run away from it all again," he said with an edge to his voice. "I get it now."

"Brad…that's not fair."

"No. It's fine. I should have seen this coming, me being cursed and all."

"I'm not running from you!" I yelled far louder than I'd intended.

"It feels a lot like that."

"I wish it didn't."

"Then stay and let's figure it out," he pleaded. "We're so close. We've narrowed it down to two people."

"Yeah, but if it's Mickey, then what? That's just…gonna be weird. And if it's Ernie? That's…"

"What's wrong with that?"

"I don't know. I wasn't expecting to feel this way. I haven't known who my dad is for so long that as I get closer, I'm suddenly…"

"Scared?"

I nodded. "Yeah."

Brad looked forlorn.

"You knew I was going to have to go back at some point. I have an apartment, a job."

"I had hoped…I don't know…that it might be different this time."

"I'm sorry." It was all I could say. I was sorry. About all of it.

Brad took the burgers from the pan, prepared them on plates with his back to me, then he slid a plate to me and stood at the counter across from me while looking as if I'd just stomped all over his heart. Because I had.

I knew it was going to be rough to tell him this, but I hadn't anticipated he'd take it this hard, or the fact that I would be alone with him, unable to get away after. I guess that was my penance—to continue to face the guy who I'd crushed not once, but twice. I had lost my appetite, but I ate a couple of bites anyway. Then I said, "I can call someone to come and get me."

"No. I'll take you home."

"Are you sure?"

"I'm sure."

****

The hills were foggy and gray as we rode back, matching the mood in the car. I kept trying to think of something to say to make it right, but everything I came up with sounded superficial. I wished it didn't have to be like this, but I couldn't stay here. He had to have known that. I loved him; I really did. But it wouldn't work. Not because of him, but because of her. This place, my family, everything I felt while I was in Alton, like I was drowning, was not something that was going to go away. I had hoped things might be different this time, but if anything, it was so much worse, especially with Grammy gone.

When he pulled into the driveway of the farm and stopped the car, I turned to him, and in almost a whisper, I offered the only conciliation I could think of. "I'll be back in a month for the wedding."

He nodded.

I got out of the car and didn't look back as I collected the hidden key from the porch swing. As the car reversed down the drive and I unlocked the door, I wondered if this would be the last time I'd ever talk to Brad Finley.

Chapter Fifteen

I slept late, though technically I hadn't done much sleeping at all. The nightmares were so much worse here. I wasn't sure if it was because I was back in my old bedroom or if it was because of what happened with Brad. When I finally got up, a light rain was coming down outside and the drafty, old farmhouse felt chilly and damp. I picked up the crocheted afghan Grammy had made me when I was little, that had been strewn over the back of the chair, and I draped it over my shoulders before going downstairs.

The house was quiet. Mom's bed was made; it appeared she hadn't slept here again. Typical. GG's door was open when I passed by, but it was almost ten, so I knew he wouldn't be in the house at this hour. The coffee pot was half full still, so I poured a cup and put it in the microwave to reheat it. When it was done, I took it, and I stood looking out the back window.

I saw Max's car parked in his usual spot. Farmers couldn't take weekends off, but that worked to my advantage because I still had to talk to him before I left tomorrow morning. I took a deep breath, feeling the heavy burden of things to come weigh upon me, and I went to the couch. When I sat down, the afghan nearly slipped from my shoulders and I hoisted it back up, wrapping it around me like a scarf. It was then that the attack began. Just like that. My vision darkened and my heart started thumping outside of my chest. I set my coffee down and extended my whole body on the sofa, closing my eyes, trying to do the breathing exercises that never worked. I began counting backwards from ten.

As I took deep inhalations through my nose and blew out my mouth, there was one thing I now could say for certain. Brad was not the trigger. He was gone, likely for good. It had to be something else. I pulled the blanket up for warmth and then I remembered something about the discussion Brad and I had recently about the first panic attack I ever experienced. I had been under this very blanket when he found me. We'd been playing hide and seek. Was there something about this specific item causing me to have anxiety? I did often associate it with Sonny. She and I loved to take our naps under our matching baby blankies when we were toddlers. My memory of that time was fuzzy at best, but there were bits and pieces, and this blanket is in a lot of them. It was the one thing I remember having before Sonny died, before Mom and I came back to the farm that I carried along with me here.

I took the blanket off and folded it up, tucking it away in the closet to see if my theory held water. After several minutes, my body began to calm. My chest was still tight, and I was left feeling even more exhausted than before, so I went back to the couch, closed my eyes, and drifted off.

When I woke up, I was surprised to find the daylight outside fading. I checked my phone. It was nearly two in the afternoon. I'd slept for much longer than I'd intended. I got up and didn't see any sign that GG had come in for lunch. I wasn't too worried because it was normal for him, but his behavior was going to have to change when I left. He couldn't be skipping meals. I looked out the back window again. The rain had stopped for the most part, but I didn't see any signs of GG on the property. I found one of Grammy's spring jackets in the coat closet and I set out in search of my grandpa. I would feel much better about all of this if I could just convince GG to start carrying a cell phone. That would have been like trying to convince a farmer to become a vegetarian. Wasn't going to happen.

Max's car was gone. Shoot. I'd missed my window to talk to him. I would have to make sure to have my mother do it. Another thing to add to the list. I went into the cow barn and when I didn't see GG at the milking post, I checked his back office. He wasn't in there either. I called out for him, but he didn't answer. Now I started to get a slightly uneasy feeling in my gut, because while the rain had let up, it was still wet as all get out, so I didn't think he was roaming the fields. Where would he be? Could he have gone with Max somewhere?

Could he be sitting in the hayloft again? It wasn't ideal weather for it, and I worried that if he was spending too much time up there, maybe he wasn't handling things as well as we all assumed he might be.

I turned the corner to check and that's when my heart stopped. GG was lying flat on his back on the hard ground below the ledge of the loft.

"GG?" I screamed and ran to him. When I got there, I went down on my knees beside him and shook him gently. His eyes were closed. "GG? Can you hear me?"

I didn't know what to do. I looked at his chest and then checked his pulse. I felt something, but it was faint. I took my phone out and dialed 911.

The operator tried to keep me calm. She asked if he

was breathing. I said I thought he was. She then said that there wasn't anything I could do now but wait until the ambulance arrived. I took his hand and squeezed it, telling him I was here, to just hold on, as tears streamed down my cheeks and landed on his.

It felt like forever, but it was likely just minutes before I heard the sirens blasting up the winding curves of the Alton hills. I didn't want to leave GG's side, but I needed to go out and wave the paramedics into the barn, or they would never find us, so I kissed his cheek and ran out.

The first person I saw headed toward me at full sprint was Ernie. He was loaded down with equipment. "Luna…is it Gus? Where is he?"

"Ernie!" I waved and pivoted. "He's in here!"

I ran back inside with Ernie at my heels. He got down and started to work and I stood back and gave him room to do so. Several more people came jogging in after and the last two to come in carried a stretcher, but by the time they were ready to load him on, Ernie had somehow managed to bring GG back around. His eyes were open and he was trying to sit up.

"Take it easy, Gus. Just stay where you are. Let us take care of you. You just relax. Keep taking nice deep breaths from this free air I brought for you, okay?" Ernie turned to wave over the two men with the stretcher, then said, "We're gonna move you over to this board exactly how you are, Gus. You don't need to move a muscle."

They transferred GG's body to the stretcher with very little effort. As they started to cart him away, Ernie took my hand and led me out. "Come on," he said. "You can ride with him in the back. I'll call your mom on the way."

"What happened? Is he going to be okay?"

"He's stable right now. We won't know more until we get him to the hospital, but he looks good. He's a tough old man. I think he'll pull through."

Ernie squeezed my hand and this time, I squeezed back.

Chapter Sixteen

They wheeled my grandfather into the ER and I was handed a stack of forms to fill out in the waiting area. I sat down with them but couldn't concentrate enough to read through them.

By that time, my mother arrived. "How is he? Did they tell you anything?"

"No. They just told me to fill these out." I handed the clipboard to her and she sat down.

Just then Ernie came out. We both stood up. "No news yet," he said.

My mother looked at me. "What happened?"

"I was looking for him because it was late and he hadn't come in for lunch. I found him just…lying there next to the bottom of the ladder." I let a sob escape before continuing. "He may have fallen off the ladder, out of the loft altogether, or it could have been something else entirely. I don't know."

"Or, he could have simply fainted," Ernie suggested. "Especially since he just lost his wife and he's clearly not been eating and drinking properly. Let's not rush to conclusions."

We both nodded and Mom sat back down. "I was worried something like this might happen," she muttered.

I looked at her and felt my blood start to warm. "*You* were worried? I was the one who told you that I was concerned, and I believe you said that he could take care of himself. I was the one who said he needed someone here to look after him and you blew me off."

"Well, you were there, so I figured that's what you were doing!"

"Okay," Ernie said. "This is not the time to point fingers, ladies. We're just lucky that Luna found him when she did. Let's all take a few deep breaths and wait to hear what the doctors have to say."

Both my mom and I nodded. She looked down and began to fill out the paperwork. I was too shaken to sit down and relax, so I decided to do some pacing of my own for GG's sake. As I walked the now familiar halls of the hospital, I was surprised at how in the matter of an hour, my entire attitude toward a person could change.

Suddenly, I realized that maybe Ernie was the hero I'd been searching for my whole life. He had saved my grandpa's life after all. And to top it off, he'd actually defended me against my mother. Twice.

Another thing he was right about was that it was a good thing that I'd been there to find GG. Who knows what might have happened if I hadn't been. Max had already gone for the day and my mother wasn't around enough to be reliable. Plus, she'd soon be living somewhere else entirely. My mom wasn't wrong, as much as I wished she was. I was the one who was supposed to be taking care of GG at that moment. I was responsible for him, and I'd failed. I'd never forgive myself if things didn't end well.

When I got back to the lobby area, I saw the ER doctor talking with Mom and Ernie. I ran up to hear what was being said, but I was too late. The doctor had already turned to retreat back through the doors.

"What did he say?"

"They're still running a few tests, but he's okay," my mother said. "Dad claimed he slipped on the ladder coming down from the hay loft and fell. That's all. The doctor said his blood sugar was a bit low, so Ernie was also probably right. He may have gotten dizzy, but you know Grandpa, he insists he just missed the rung. Anyway, he has a broken ankle, and they want to keep him overnight for observation and for the additional tests to come back before they release him."

I looked at Ernie for reassurance. He nodded. "I think he'll be alright."

I breathed out a huge sigh of relief. "Can we see him?"

"Yes. The doctor said we can go back for a few minutes."

I headed back and threw my arms around GG the second I saw that he was alert. His ankle was wrapped in a bandage. "You gave me quite a scare."

"It wasn't me," he said. "It was the damn ladder. Knocked the wind out of me."

"Well, I'm just glad you're okay."

"Nothing to worry about," he said.

"You should have come in for some lunch," I scolded.

"I wasn't hungry. Had a big breakfast."

"Okay," Ernie said. "Let's not get too worked up."

"Ernie fixed you up," I said. "He was amazing. You should have seen him." I turned toward him to show him how truly grateful I was.

He blushed. "Just doing my job."

My mother cleared her throat. "All's well that ends well. We should probably get out of here now and let you rest, Dad. We'll keep in touch with the doctor."

"Okay," he said.

I squeezed him again, much to his chagrin, and then I followed Mom and Ernie out.

Back out in the lobby, we ran straight into Max as he rushed in. "What happened?"

Ernie explained while Mom took my arm and pulled me away. "I've got to get back to work. What are your plans?"

"I'm supposed to leave in the morning, but…I don't see how I can do that now."

"Why not?"

"I just…don't want this type of thing to happen to him again. You were right. This was my fault. I…"

I couldn't help it, but it had all caught up with me and I lost it. As I cried, my mother looked…uncomfortable with my display. She said, "Luna, for heaven's sake. Your grandfather is going to be fine." She pulled a tissue from her purse and handed it to me.

"Thanks to Ernie," I said between sniffles.

"Yes. Thanks to Ernie," she agreed. "Why don't you go back to the farm and pack."

"I don't have my car."

"Where is it?"

I had to think. "In the parking lot of Finley's Bar."

She shook her head as if she was disgusted with me. "I don't have time for this. We have a private gallery showing tonight. Ask Ernie if he can drop you there."

"Isn't anybody going to stay with GG?"

"The doctor has my number. He said he'd call when he knew more."

"Okay."

She turned, and without saying goodbye to Ernie or Max, headed out the doors of the ER as if it was just another day and she had things to do. It did not shock me. I was sure her boss at the art gallery would have been understanding if she had said that her father was in the ER because he'd almost died, but that wasn't in my mother's DNA. If something difficult was happening, she was more likely to get away from it with the speed of a bullet train than stay to handle the fallout.

Ernie was still talking to Max, so I fell back into the waiting room chair with the heavy notion that one of the reasons I did not like my mother was because I kept seeing things in her...that reflected back onto me. Like how we both ran away from hard things.

I'd spent my whole life trying to be everything my mother was not, but in the last week, I'd come to find that I was more like her than I ever thought possible and it made me feel horrible about myself. Because when I looked at her, I saw a selfish person who did not know how to express her feelings in a positive manner. Instead of giving affection, she went cold.

Could that be me, as well? Was I an awful person? Afraid to stay or get attached to anyone because it was overly complicated? I had always attributed my mother's inability to nurture to her fragile mental state, but what if that was just who she was? And what if it was who I was too?

"Luna?"

I glanced up and found Max and Ernie standing in front of me.

"Everything okay?" Ernie asked.

I must have had a horrifying expression on my face that came with the horrifying reality of my existence.

"Yeah. Fine," I muttered. "I'm still just a little flustered."

"I'm so sorry I wasn't there," Max said.

I shook my head. "It's not your fault."

"It wasn't anybody's fault," Ernie said.

"Please let me know if there's anything I can do," Max offered. "And call me if anything changes."

"We will," Ernie said.

After Max left, I turned to Ernie. "Mom said you might be able to drive me to my car, but I just remembered that you got here the same way I did...by ambulance."

Ernie checked his phone. "And they took it back to the station. I can call someone and have them come and get us."

As we waited, I felt lightheaded myself. It wasn't anxiety this time. It was nearly five thirty. I hadn't eaten anything since the night before at Brad's place. Here I was scolding GG and I was doing the same thing as him. I could tell that my own blood sugar was low now that my adrenaline had finally calmed down.

Ernie's colleague, a nice-looking guy maybe a little younger than me, dropped us in the parking lot of Finley's. Ernie thanked him. I handed him the keys to the rental car and asked if he minded driving as I was feeling a little woozy and I had a tension headache.

He paused just outside the car. "We should get you some food. Want to go inside?"

"The bar?" We both turned and looked toward it.

"Sure. Why not?"

"Uh…" I paused, trying to think of a rational excuse for why I didn't want to go inside that particular place. "It looks kind of crowded. Could we go somewhere a little quieter? I'm still pretty overwhelmed by the stress of the day."

"Okay. Sure," he said.

"My treat this time. I want to pay you back somehow for saving GG's life."

"Aw, shucks. I was just doing my job, but I won't say no to a meal. Let's do it," he said.

"Great!"

Chapter Seventeen

Ernie took us just outside of Alton to a little café that served breakfast all day. It was off the beaten path and exactly what I'd asked for: quiet. Likely because it was kind of a dump. The floors had a sheen that I didn't think was polish but a thin layer of grease. The place was probably empty because the windows were so filthy it almost looked like they were closed from the outside. A lack of customers during the dinner rush on a Saturday night spoke volumes. At least the service would hopefully be fast, and fast was all I required at this point because I was desperate to get something in my belly.

We sat tucked away in a booth toward the back of the joint and a woman nearly as old as Grammy came out to hand us plastic menus. I went ahead and ordered something safe, knowing the food might not be great. I chose pancakes and a decaf tea, while Ernie, obviously less bothered by the cleanliness factor of the place, got steak and eggs.

She brought us back our drinks quickly, and I clutched my mug across from Ernie and took a minute to really examine his facial features trying to discern whether or not I resembled him in any way, shape, or form. If I was being honest, there were some similarities. We both had green eyes and sort of bulbous noses. Our skin tones were equal shades of pale. While he wore glasses, I used contacts. We were both fairly short and I certainly wasn't as thin as my mother. I wondered what color his hair would be if he had any, but I guessed it would match the light shading of his brows that were visible over the top of his glasses. Same shade as my own hair color.

I had little doubt at this point about him being my dad. And even though my impression of him had changed drastically in the last eight hours or so, I still was on the fence about whether or not I wanted to be told outright that it was true. I was curious. If he were prodded, would he confess? Did he even know? What if he didn't? How would he react if I brought it up?

I took a sip of my steaming tea, and said, "I saw Diana Butcher a few days ago. Do you know her?"

"Sure. She was friends with my sister back in the day."

"Uh huh. She mentioned that. She also told me that you and Mom went to your senior prom together," I said and gave him a questioning look.

Our eyes met briefly before he lowered his gaze. "That's true." He took a sip of his water.

"What happened?"

He nearly choked on his drink. He didn't answer because he was saved by the server bringing us our food. I'd been right about the speedy factor. It was the one thing this place had going for it. The food looked pale and unappetizing, but it was hot. Ernie dug into his like a starving orphan.

I said, "What I meant was…why did you and Mom stop seeing one another back then?"

"We weren't a couple. Not really. I asked her to the dance and she said yes. It was a date."

"Just the one time?"

He nodded. "I liked your mother very much, but I didn't get the sense that it was mutual at the time."

"But she went to the prom with you?"

"She did." He said as if he were still that hopeful teenage boy who'd been crushed. He focused once again on the plate of food in front of him. His body language made it apparent that he wasn't interested in talking about this anymore, and while I was curious to know why that was, I dropped it for the time being.

I focused my attention on my own plate of food. The pancakes were dry even with butter and syrup soaked into them, but I wasn't going to complain about it. Each bite eased my pounding head a little more, and my wariness began fading.

Ernie soaked up some of his running egg with a thick slab of Texas toast, the best looking thing on the plate by a mile. "Your mother said you're leaving tomorrow?"

"That was the plan, but I'm not sure now."

"It would be good if you could stick around." He shot me a quick grin and I wondered if that was how a proud father might look at his daughter.

"Yeah. I mean with everything happening, I think it might be for the best if I stayed to help."

He nodded and I thought we were on the same page. In fact, I marveled at how easy it was to communicate with him. Then he said, "Your mother could really use your help."

"My mother?"

"Yeah. To assist her with the wedding stuff. Lots of planning and arranging to do in a short period of time." He laughed. "She has a list longer than Santa's."

"Actually, I was talking about staying to take care

of GG."

"Well, sure. But I know it would really make Jennifer happy to have you around more."

"I'm not so sure about that."

"No. It's true."

"Then why has she asked me about a dozen times when I'm leaving?"

"You know her. She's just being motherly."

I cocked my head to the side. "Uh huh. Cause she's always been so *motherly*."

He raised his brow. "I know you two haven't always seen eye-to-eye, but you should give her a chance. She really loves you."

"She doesn't do a great job of showing it," I said.

"Well, maybe if you stick around, she'll do better."

"If I stick around," I said, sharply, "it will be for my grandpa. The person who actually raised me."

His face, the one I'd only seen be soft up until now, hardened. "You think you know everything, but you don't give your mom enough respect. You don't know everything she went through, everything she did was because she loved you."

"Do you?" I asked. "Know everything she went through?"

"I know enough."

"Then you know that she will have days when she won't let you turn the light on because she claims it's too much for her? You know that she will sometimes stop in the middle of normal conversation, throw herself on the ground, curl up, and not move for a solid four hours? You know that she will begin to scream in the shower and have to be talked out of the tub so she doesn't drown?"

125

"Yes. I've been made aware of all that, but she's doing well now," he said with a twinge of doubt. "You haven't given her a chance. I know you look at her and think she's the same woman you left ten years ago, but she's not."

"I've been here for a whole week," I argued. "I see a woman who is temporarily happy because of a newfound love, but…what about when that fades?"

He shook his head. "That's not really your problem, is it?"

"Isn't it?"

"You're turning things back on me, but I'm not worried about that and you shouldn't be either. You should be trying to repair your relationship with her."

"I…think if that were going to happen, it would have by now."

"You have to want it, too."

"You think I don't want my own mother to love me? That's all I've ever wanted."

"I don't want to argue with you, Luna. But, as an impartial observer, I can see your wall and you've built a pretty damn high fortress around yourself. It's almost impenetrable. I understand the need to protect yourself, but this is your family. Your mother."

I laughed. "You think you're impartial? The man who plans to marry her?"

"Okay, okay. Maybe I'm not impartial, but I am trying. Look…all I know is what your mom tells me, and she has made it abundantly clear that she loves you more than anything. She wishes things could be different."

"Why hasn't she ever made it abundantly clear to me then?"

He didn't have an answer. Nor did I. We finished

our meals in awkward silence, and I drove Ernie back to his house, a mid-sized A-frame nestled deep in the trees. This was the place that my mother would soon be living. That annoyed me for various reasons, but mostly because it looked like a lovely cabin retreat. I'd always thought of myself as a city dweller, but since being back in Alton, a nice hideout in the woods away from everyone and everything was sounding better and better to me.

I stopped the car and didn't speak. I was still reeling from our conversation. Before he got out, he turned to me and said, "Thank you for dinner. I enjoyed spending time with you. I know you didn't like hearing what I had to say but you've been sheltered your whole life, protected from the hard stuff, whether or not you chose to see that. Even though our conversation was hard, we needed to have it. We're family now."

"Not yet," I said. "And the way I know that is because nobody in my family would have said any of the things you said to me tonight."

"Right. And maybe it's exactly what you've needed to hear."

Before I could respond, he got out of the car and slammed the door shut.

Chapter Eighteen

I wanted to blame the thirty-year-old bed mattress for how uncomfortable I was, but it probably wasn't the culprit for why I couldn't sleep. I lay awake stewing about what Ernie had said to me. I was angry. What did this guy know about my family? Who was he to tell me that I had a wall up? I'd only seen the guy a handful of times. He knew nothing about me.

And yet, he apparently had a fairly firm understanding of my mother. In some ways, he may have understood her better than I did. This was new for me. I wasn't sure what to make of any of it. I wanted to fight. I wanted to make them call this ridiculous wedding off, but there was another part of me that was glad someone else would be shouldering the burden of my mother. That it no longer fell to me was a relief.

Because, if I couldn't fight, I desperately wanted to take flight. But that was no longer an option either. Not after what happened to my grandpa. So, when the rooster crowed, I got up out of my childhood bed, canceled my flight, and I headed to the hospital to retrieve GG and bring him back to the farm.

He'd been moved into a different room and I was allowed to go sit with him while we waited for him to be discharged. I could see that he was getting restless with each minute that ticked by. I wanted to get out of there too, but we were at the mercy of the doctor.

A nurse came in and offered him some breakfast. GG said, "Nope. We're leaving soon."

I gave him a look. "This is what got you here in the first place, remember?"

"Could still be a bit of a wait," she said, calmly. "Doctor Swenson has to sign off on the release forms before you can go and he's running a little behind on his rounds this morning."

GG groaned.

"Might as well eat while you're waiting," the nurse said.

He shrugged and I thanked the nurse.

She brought in a tray of food that looked about as appetizing as the stuff they'd served at the café the night before. Some watery oatmeal and half a grapefruit sat on the center of the tray. A small plate with a stack of white toast was off to the side.

"How about a piece of toast?" I asked him. "Can't screw up toast."

"Sure, but only if you share it with me," he said.

"Deal."

I was about to butter it when he slapped my hand away. "It's my turn to butter."

He handed me half a piece of buttered toast.

I pushed the orange juice toward him. He slid it back to me. "You drink that. I'll have the milk."

"Deal." We clinked the small glasses together and chuckled before we drank them down.

Eventually the doctor came in, looking down, reading through paperwork on a clipboard in front of him. He finished flipping through the documents and looked up. "Okay. Mr. Andersen, all of the labs came back looking good. You still feeling well this morning?"

"Fit as a fiddle. Can I go?"

He signed the forms and said, looking at me, "I'd recommend having someone keep an eye on him for a couple more days just to be sure."

"That's exactly what I plan to do," I said.

"Good. Not that he'll get far with his ankle in that brace."

The doctor and I laughed and GG silently stewed. "No walking or putting pressure on that foot of any kind."

"Got that GG?" I asked.

He grunted.

"There's more information in this paperwork here," the doctor said, handing me a packet. "He'll need to go to the clinic to get it set in a cast in a few days, when the swelling goes down a bit more."

"Okay."

"Otherwise, unless you have any questions, you're free to go."

"Let's go," GG muttered. Being confined like this and relying upon another person was torturing his pacing soul.

"Thanks so much," I said to the doctor. It was almost noon by the time we were finally out of there. As I pushed GG down the last stretch of hallway in the wheelchair, we rounded the corner and were almost to the front door when my mother burst through them. Oh," she said, stopping in front of us. "They discharged you already?"

"Already?" he said. "I said first thing in the morning to you on the telephone!"

"Hospitals move at a snail's pace," she argued. "Especially on a Sunday. I'm shocked you're ready to go."

"I can take him back, if you help me get him in the car," I said to her.

She agreed.

Once he was safely buckled into the passenger seat and I closed the door, my mother collapsed the wheelchair the hospital loaned us and started to load it in the trunk. "Ernie told me you've decided to stay."

"For a while, anyway," I said.

"I hope it's not because you feel guilty."

"No. It's because it's the right thing to do."

She closed the trunk. "Okay, well, thank you for taking him home."

"Again, I'm not doing it for you."

She rolled her eyes. "Goodbye, Luna."

I got in and GG and I drove back to the farm. Halfway there, he said, "what did you mean when you told the doctor you were gonna keep an eye on me? I thought you were leaving today?"

"I changed my mind."

"Why? Because of me? Lu, I really did just trip coming down the ladder."

"It's not because of you," I said. I knew if I told him it was because of him, he'd be more cranky than he already was. "Mom needs help…with the wedding stuff. Besides, I've been meaning to make the transition to full-time freelance illustrator for a while now. My rent is too expensive in New York to do that, and you said the farm was my home and I could stay if I wanted. So, can I?"

"If you want," he said with a shrug. "Under one condition…"

"What's that?"

"I like a little more butter on my sandwiches."

I smiled. "I can do that."

"Then you can stay."

"Can I have a condition too?" I asked.

"Maybe. It depends on what it is."

"I have to return this rental car soon, so I won't have anything to drive. The mechanic sent a text message that the truck's ready to be picked up."

"You want to drive my truck?"

"I'm not sure how else you plan to get to the clinic next week to get your cast put on."

"Eh, it's just a sprain. Doesn't need a cast."

"I can have Mom take you, if you'd prefer," I counter-offered.

"You promise not to break my truck again?" he teased.

"Promise."

"Okay. It's a deal."

I glanced over at him and he gave me a playful wink.

Chapter Nineteen

I unpacked my bags again, this time putting them away in my childhood dresser. It was surreal. I talked to my boss and the company agreed to let me work my last few weeks remotely. I still had another month on my apartment lease, which was fine because it gave me some time before I needed to get back there and pack all of my stuff up. Since GG couldn't go up the stairs, I unfolded the hide-a-bed in the couch in the small den off of the living room. The den had been mostly utilized as Grammy's sewing room, but it would work for the short term.

GG and I were figuring out how to live together again. It was much different this time because Grammy wasn't here to guide us, and also because GG couldn't get away. He was stuck inside the house unless I wheeled him out to check on things, which he wanted to do often.

Mom popped in now and again, so at least that aspect of things hadn't changed at all. Having had a little time to let my conversation with Ernie settle, while I still wasn't willing to accept that everything he said was right, I did wonder if I had a wall up. I figured it wouldn't kill me to be a little softer with my mother when I did see her, giving her the benefit of the doubt when my instinct was to shout and lose my patience with her.

She and I even sat down one afternoon to work on some wedding plans. She pulled out a legal pad with a million things written on it. She went over some of her thoughts with me, and to my shock, we managed to get a few things accomplished without murdering one another in the process. We discussed food options, music, and I said I'd call around about flowers.

While she made note of it on her pad of paper, I said, "Mom, are you one hundred percent sure that you want to do this?"

"Do what, dear?"

"Marry Ernie."

"Of course, I'm sure. Why wouldn't I be?"

"I'm just checking."

She went back to her sheet for a minute, staring at it, and then she looked at me. "I've never been happier. Honestly. I wish you'd give him a chance."

I almost snorted. It was like they'd rehearsed the same speech, only with the other person's name swapped out. Instead, I simply shrugged. "He's fine."

"He's a good man. And he would really like to have a relationship with you."

"Why?" I asked her.

"Why? Because he's going to be part of the family."

I knew asking my mother straight if Ernie was my biological dad wouldn't yield results at this point, so I went around it. I was always trying to catch her in a bluff or get her to accidentally tell me things, but she was too cunning for these things. That, or I was terrible at them. Probably the latter. Most likely, the latter.

"Has he been married before?" I asked her.

"No."

"Why not?"

"Well, he went off to college and then he got sidetracked, so…"

"Sidetracked? He told me that he decided he hated it there and realized business wasn't for him."

"Well, yes. That was part of it, but...really, he came home to care for his parents. His father was ill with Parkinson's disease. It was quite difficult for his mother to face, and while he cared for his dad's physical ailments, Martha started to slide mentally."

"That's too bad," I said.

"Yes. He thought he could care for them both, but it proved to be too much for everyone, so he had to check his mother into a mental facility for a bit. It was very hard on him. He didn't have time to focus on himself. And then when his father passed, he brought his mother back to the house and they worked through everything. She's doing well now."

"Oh."

"And that was when he realized that he enjoyed helping people, so he began training to be a paramedic."

"I see."

"So, does that answer your question?" I nodded.

As she was packing her bag up to head out, she said, "If you'd like, you can use my bedroom as your office. I've got most of my things out of there at this point."

"Really? That would be great, actually."

"There's a small desk in the garage. Max can help you move in. It's my old one, but I had it restored recently. I was thinking of moving it to Ernie's, but there's really no space for it."

"Thanks."

So, later that day, while GG was napping, I set out to find Max and ask him about the desk. I caught him at a good time between tasks, and the two of us were able to carry the desk inside, up the steps, and put it in Mom's bedroom which was now virtually empty.

"Thank you," I said.

"No problem. It looks nice in here."

"Yeah. It will come in handy since I'll be working from here now."

He nodded. "Whole town's buzzing about you being back for good."

I laughed. "I doubt that very much."

"I hate to get involved with you kids, but..." he hesitated. "Are you and Brad on the outs?"

My stomach twisted. "I don't want to be, but I did what I do best—I screwed things up between us."

"I don't know what transpired between you, but, one thing about Brad, he doesn't hold a grudge."

"I know. He's one of the good ones."

"I'm just a simple farmhand," Max said, "so I don't know much, but you'd have to be blind to not see how much he cares about you."

"I care about him too, but I'm not sure if this can be fixed."

"Listen, I try not to butt into my son's affairs, but I'm guessing he'd be willing to clear the air. I'd given him a chance."

I wanted to tell Max that it wasn't about giving Brad a chance. He wasn't the problem. It was me. But how could I look at this sweet man and tell him that? I didn't want him to be disappointed in me, so I said I'd think about it, and we left it at that. I thanked him again for helping me. He tipped his cowboy hat and left.

I sat down at the desk, which was a lovely, dark-wood rolltop. It was not lost on me that it was the second time in one week that I was told to give someone a chance. Did I not usually do that? I hadn't thought of myself as someone who held others at arm's length, except, it was becoming more and more apparent that it was exactly what I did. Ernie had told me that I had a wall up. It made sense for me to have a wall up with my mother. She'd hurt me over and over again.

But, Brad? He'd never done a thing to make me want to build a wall around him and yet, maybe I had. Why? I suppose it was because I was scared of being hurt by him too. He was the one person who I actually had a solid foundation with and the idea of it crumbling down was not something I wanted. Yet, it was already crumbled. I'd done that. I couldn't possibly keep subjecting him to my instability. It was why I'd avoided relationships altogether. I was damaged, broken, exactly as I told him on the beach.

I ran my hand along the edge of the roll top and I lifted it up to reveal a flat surface. There was a small drawer on the right side that I pulled out. To my surprise, a small sketch pad was tucked inside. It was familiar looking. It looked exactly like the one I used as a little girl and kept in my top drawer. I thought I'd seen that one on the reference shelf downstairs recently. Why would it be here now?

I pulled it out and flipped it open. I expected to see my old doodles of puppies and kitties, rainbows, and unicorns. I spent hours drawing when I was a little girl. It took me to another place away from my loneliness. It was cathartic, the only therapy I had for what I was feeling at the time. I wasn't very good, having had no special training or guidance beyond the few books Grammy had purchased for me.

The doodles here on the first few pages were not ones I recalled doing. In fact, they didn't look like something I could have done. They were much, much better than anything my skills could have produced at the time. And the subject matter was far more mature. They were of trees and lifelike birds. They weren't cartoony looking, but very realistic.

I turned the page to find a short poem written on it.

Combine
We were one,
Until we were none.
I—your protector,
You—mine.
I let you down,
No longer combined.
Harsh and swift,
The metal tendrils spun.
Thrashing.
Cutting.
Until they were done.

****

I recognized the printing immediately. This was my mother's writing. The poem seemed to be about her brother Robbie who had been killed in the farm accident.

I was once again floored by my mother's writing. It hit me right in the gut. It was subtle, yet so devastatingly beautiful, just like the poem she'd written for Grammy. My mother's creative abilities, a complete mystery to me until a week ago, astounded me. I knew she'd gone to the university with the intention of becoming an artist, but I just thought that was a random choice, something she liked the idea of rather than something she actually loved and had a passion for. I never believed she was artistic because I had never seen it. Now I saw that I was dead wrong about that. And if I was wrong about that, what else was I wrong about?

Now, as I flipped the pages faster, it was like I was seeing my mom in a new light. The sketches and snippets of writing from her youth were mature and beautiful. It was like I was seeing an entirely different person through this lens.

As I got close to the end of the pages, a small piece of unattached paper came loose and floated to the floor. I picked it up gently so I didn't tear it as I could see that it was yellowing and fragile. Torn at the edges, it appeared to be old newsprint. I turned it over and read:

Police were called to an apartment in NE Minneapolis on the evening of March 12th after neighbors reported hearing a loud argument and then a subsequent gunshot. A four-year-old child was pronounced dead at the scene. Jeffrey Donovan, the alleged shooter, was taken into custody. It's unclear what led to the argument and police are not releasing the name of the child at this time. They are investigating it as an attempted break-in, possibly connected to a local biker gang.

****

I read it over a few more times trying to understand. The only thing I knew for sure was that March *12th* was the date my twin sister died.

"Lu?" GG called from downstairs. "Are you busy?"

"Coming!"

I tucked the clipping back into the sketch pad and went downstairs.

"Gotta use the loo, Lu," he joked.

We were lucky that there was a half-bath on the main floor, but it was a tight squeeze and the wheelchair wouldn't fit in the door. I had to help GG out of the chair outside the door, and hand him his cane. The system worked, but it wasn't something he could do alone.

After helping GG get to the bathroom, I made him some dinner. After that, we took a short stroll around the property as the sun set. The nights were getting warmer, so I wheeled GG to a spot on the front porch and he sat reading the paper while smoking his evening pipe.

I plopped down on the swing beside him and stared off listening to the crickets. Now that I had a moment to redirect my thoughts, they went back to the newspaper clipping. I had never heard the name Jeffrey Donovan before. So this was the person who killed Sonny. Why had neighbors heard an argument? And why would a biker gang be robbing people? I had a strange thought. Was there more to this story than just a simple break-in.

"GG? Do you know which days Mom works at the art gallery?"

"I believe it's Wednesdays, Fridays, and some Saturdays."

"I might head over there tomorrow for a little while if you're okay here. I've been meaning to check the place out."

"I'll be fine," he said. "Don't need to worry about me."

"Unless you need to use the bathroom," I reminded him. "I'll ask Max to pop in while I'm gone."

GG gave a grunt and went back to his reading. We sat outside until the mosquitos became unrelenting and the light got too thin for GG to see his paper. I helped him get ready for bed and he retired to the den. I went upstairs and sat down at my mother's old desk again. I Googled Jeffrey Donovan's name. There were some hits on a sculptor who lived and worked in NYC. An artist?

Could this be the guy? I thought he was in a biker gang? It was curious that he was also an artist. One of the hits on the search was an advertisement for a gallery exhibit and it included what appeared to be a recent photo.

He stood next to an abstract metal sculpture. He wasn't smiling, but he didn't look evil, not like a man who could murder a child anyway. Uncomfortable would be the word I would use to describe what he looked like, maybe a bit shy and awkward. His hands were pushed deep into his jeans and his head was tilted slightly. He wasn't overly tall or short. Not too thin or thick. His hair was short. He was sort of average looking.

Maybe this wasn't him. But maybe it was.

I sat for the next hour or so and dug through every last thing I could find online about him. I stumbled upon a personal website for his art. There were several professional looking photos of large scale pieces of artwork for sale. They were all abstract and his medium tended to be metal though a few were of more pliable materials. They were interesting, but I wasn't sure I was enamored with them.

There wasn't much listed under his bio; it was sort of generic, mostly talking about how he'd always been passionate about art and how he started sculpting after he received a bag of pipe cleaners to make a craft project in elementary school.

An email address was listed under his contact info. If this was the right person, I was looking at a way to get in touch with him. If I wasn't able to get anything out of my mother, this would be my plan *B*. I was hoping I wouldn't have to email a stranger asking if he killed my sister and why, but I would if I had to.

Not surprisingly, when I finally fell into my bed, I

barely slept. It was hard to not be unsettled by things. Once again, my truths had been ripped wide open and I lay there trying to piece them back together. I knew that if I wanted my mother to unlock her vault, this time I needed to go in with more fight than I'd put up the last time. It was unfortunate that it was coming at a time when my mother and I had finally begun to make some good progress toward the semblance of a normal mother-daughter relationship. But I had to know what was real. It was time to find out why Sonny died and why it seemed to happen at the hands of a man who my mother may have known. Because it could not be a coincidence that she was studying art and this person also happened to be another artist.

This felt significant. In fact, it was huge. And I wasn't going to just let it go. I was going to have to go in there and demand that my mother tell me everything she knew because it seemed to me that she was hiding something. I just wasn't sure what. Or why. All I knew was that this could be my one chance to catch her and get her to divulge her secrets.

Chapter Twenty

While GG took his afternoon nap, I drove the truck to Saltwater. Saltwater was the epitome of a tourist town. It was the largest town on the river about a fifteen minute drive north from Alton. It had a storybook main street that was lined with upscale boutiques, cafes, and galleries. It was amusing to me that the town was called Saltwater and it sat along the banks of a river that did not contain a lick of salt. The closest thing containing saltwater in these parts was probably all of the taffy being sold in the candy shops along the main street.

Saltwater could not have been more different from Alton. It was glitz and glamor and there wasn't a single home that looked to belong to a working-class family. Most of the houses lining the streets outside of Main Street were the massive Queen Anne style.

It took forever to find a place to park within a feasible walking distance to the gallery. I circled and circled waiting for someone to leave a spot. The public lots were so jam packed, it didn't even seem worth trying to wait for a space to open up within them. Eventually, I got an off street space and had to try to parallel park GG's pick-up into a spot that was honestly probably too small for the vehicle I was trying to wedge in, but my patience had worn thin.

I had to walk nearly six blocks after I parked. By the time I reached the gallery, I was sweating and frazzled. I purposely decided to speak to my mother in this location because I knew that she wouldn't be able to act up. She would need to stay even and professional and she wouldn't be able to melt down or walk out on me, not unless she wanted others to see, which I knew she would not. I saw how she acted with the woman who approached us at the restaurant. That was who I was hoping my mother would be today. Stable and calm. Mature and forthcoming.

I hadn't told her that I was coming. Another genius tactic. She was unprepared for what I had in store. The galley was in a prime location, wedged between Darla's Chocolate Truffles and Vera's Old-fashioned Candy Shoppe. It was late afternoon on a Wednesday though and I could see from the glass wall that was the front of the shop that there were no other customers inside. That was also what I was hoping for. I wanted my mother to be in a public space without any members of the public directly around.

I took a deep breath and entered. I didn't see my mother, but another woman, presumably the gallery owner, was sitting behind a small desk toward the back of the room. She looked up and smiled at me. What little hope I'd felt about this mission was quickly sucked from me. I hadn't anticipated another person to be working at the gallery alongside my mother. Was this store so busy selling paintings that it needed two employees on the clock?

Of course, my mother didn't appear to be here, so what did that mean? Was she lying about her job here too? It shouldn't have surprised me. I considered turning and leaving, but I'd just spent twenty minutes finding a parking spot and walking, so I decided to check out the work. Maybe I could get a little information out of this other woman.

I began to look at the artwork that lined the walls of the space. Most of it was exactly what I'd expect to see in a tourist gallery in this area. It was very generic, over the couch pieces. The third piece I came to was a bit different. I stood examining the details of it for a long time. It was an oil landscape. The colors were muted, but also bold. Something about the design looked familiar to me, but I couldn't exactly place it. As an illustrator, I studied a lot of art in college, and I followed many current painters' work but I wasn't sure where I'd seen this style before exactly. My obvious interest in the piece must have attracted the gallery owner's attention because she'd gotten up and was suddenly standing beside me.

"This is an exceptional piece, don't you think? I just love the sky and the trees."

I turned toward her. "It's lovely. Who is the artist?"

"A local woman, believe it or not. Her name is Jennifer Andersen."

That was why it looked familiar. My mother had already begun to hone her style in her early sketch book, the one I'd found the day before. I could see it now. This was my chance to ask more questions about my mother. As I opened my mouth to do so, I was interrupted.

"Luna? What are you doing here?" My mother had emerged from the back room and was coming toward me with fury.

"Oh...here she is now," the gallery owner said. "You know her?"

"She's my mother," I said, awkwardly.

My mother stopped and composed herself. "Sandy, this is my daughter. She's an illustrator herself. She's visiting from New York. Sandy is the owner of the gallery," she said to me.

"Well, it's very nice to meet you," Sandy said before retreating to her desk at the back of the room.

When she was gone, my mother hissed at me. "What are you doing?"

I turned back to her piece. "You painted this?"

Flustered, she said, "Yes."

"It's really beautiful."

"Thank you."

"I had no idea you could do this."

"Yes, well."

"I have to talk to you about something," I said, remembering the mission.

"Now?"

"Yes."

She looked back at her boss. "I'm off in fifteen minutes. Meet me at the Waterfront Café. It's a block off of main near the river."

I hadn't expected her to agree. In fact, I was thrown off by just about everything that had happened since I had walked in, but a busy café along the would serve the purpose I needed it to, so I nodded, said goodbye to Sandy, and I shuffled out the door.

I grabbed a table outside and sat staring at the water, trying to refocus my thoughts on what I had to do. When the server came by, I ordered two glasses of wine and when she brought them back, I paid for them in case I bailed at some point during the discussion, knowing that was a strong possibility. Then, I downed most of my glass while reading the newspaper clipping over again for the millionth time. When my mother joined me, I handed her the piece of paper.

"What is this?" she asked.

"That's what I came to ask you."

With the paper firmly in her hand now, I watched her face carefully as she became aware of what she was looking at. Her features sank as if she'd seen a ghost.

"Is Jeffery Donovan my father?" I asked.

She didn't answer, so I said what I'd lain awake the night before rehearsing. "Okay. Well, I looked him up. It appears that he lives in Brooklyn of all places. So, when I'm back in the city in a few weeks to pack up my apartment, maybe I'll send Jeff a quick email and ask to meet up with him. Maybe he'll tell me the truth."

She crumpled the news clipping into a ball in her hand, and she sighed deeply. "Luna, honey, it was an awful thing that happened."

I waited for more.

My mother took a long drink of her wine and closed her eyes. Then she said, "Someone was trying to break in. I'd told you and Sonny to both stay in your bed. You listened. Sonny did not. She startled him."

"Who is he? Why was he breaking in? What did he want?"

"I don't know, Luna. I didn't ask him. He had a gun."

"Did you know him? The man I found on the internet is an artist…"

"Lots of people in that building were artists. We lived in the artist quarters near the art building on campus."

"What was the argument about?"

"Argument? Well, there was yelling. I screamed obviously. The man from down the hall came running. It all happened so fast. I…" Her hands went to her temples and I was worried I had pushed her too far.

"Are you okay?"

She turned to me directly, and the look she gave me shredded me. For the first time, I saw something in her expression, something akin to guilt, remorse, sadness. Real emotions. Something I'd longed to share with my mother since the day my twin sister was killed in cold blood. I wanted to reach out to touch her, but it wasn't something I'd ever done before. I wasn't sure how she would react to it and I didn't want to risk tipping her over the edge of the cliff.

"Are we finished talking about this now?" she asked.

I didn't want to be. I still had questions, but I knew better than to keep pushing things with her. "Yes."

She nodded.

I got up. "I have to get back to GG. Finish your wine. It's paid for."

I walked away, but for the first time, I wasn't angry with her. I actually felt bad for her.

On the drive back to the farm, my emotions flipped and settled on disappointment. I hadn't learned any more details from my mother than what I'd gotten from reading the clipping the first time. Really, all I had was a name. The name of the man who killed my sister. It was more than I'd had before, but it still didn't resolve anything for me. In fact, after talking with my mother, I had even more questions. If he was an artist, why did the paper say he was in a biker gang? It still didn't tell me why he'd busted in. The only thing I knew was that he'd been startled by my sister.

I searched my brain trying to recall anything from that night. I was also four years old, and while I had plenty of memories from that time, living in that apartment, the old lady who babysat us and watched game shows on the television, things like that, I did not recall a thing from the night my sister was shot in our living room. It was hard for me to believe I could have slept through such a thing, but I must have. The only thing I remember was the blood that remained on the wall after it happened. I and my mother left the apartment a few days later. That's when she dropped me off at the farm.

Chapter Twenty-One

The next morning, I got up early to take GG to his doctor's appointment. The sleepless nights were stacking up and taking a toll, but I couldn't let my grandpa down. We got in the truck and drove over to the clinic so he could get a cast on his ankle. He was excited because it meant he could ditch the wheelchair and start walking again on his own with the aid of just the cane.

"You feeling okay?" he asked me on the drive. "You're quiet and you look like hell."

"Yeah. Sorry. Just haven't been sleeping well."

"Is this because of that boy? Max's son?"

"No. Well, sort of."

"You like him?"

"I…don't know. It's complicated."

"Did you know that your gramma almost married a different man?"

I turned to him briefly. "What? I've never heard that before."

"Well, no. Because she came to her senses."

"What happened?"

"Her parents didn't like me."

"Why not?"

"I'm Swedish; They were Germans. That was a big deal then. But the bigger issue was that I'm just a simpleton farmer. They were educated folk. They thought Ida should be with someone smarter, more upstanding."

"Really? She disobeyed them?"

"She couldn't resist my charm," he said with a wink.

"And what does this have to do with Brad exactly? You think I don't want to be with him because you don't like him?"

"You could do better for yourself," he said.

I snorted.

We got into the clinic six minutes late. GG let every single person in that place know that it was my fault. He thought he was funny. I wasn't in the mood. And it didn't matter because we waited forever before he was called back. I wheeled him to the room. I was going to return to the waiting area while he got his cast set, when a woman with blaze orange hair and a white lab coat walked in.

She was looking down at her clipboard reading over her notes.

"Fia?" I said.

She looked up and smiled. "Luna!"

She was no longer the skinny, fire-engine-red-haired girl with oversized glasses and freckles. Her skin was creamy, and her hair had softened into the most magnificent orange waves. She was stunningly gorgeous. And a doctor. We hugged. "It's so great to see you."

"Your mom told me you worked here, but I'd completely forgotten," I said.

"You saw my mom?"

"Yeah. She actually gave me your number."

"What? Why didn't you call me?"

"I was planning to, but I hadn't gotten around to it yet."

"I'm here too," GG said from his wheelchair.

Fia looked down at him. "Hello, Gus. It's nice to see you. I hear you fell off of a ladder."

"The ladder pushed me!"

She laughed. "Either way, let's take a look."

While she unwrapped the bandage, she said to me, "Hey, I'm having a small dinner party tomorrow night at my place. I'd love for you to come."

"Oh, I don't want to intrude," I said.

"You won't be. It's just a few friends. I want you to meet my husband and kids."

"Kids?"

"Yeah. Believe it or not, I have three."

"Three kids? Wow!"

"Please come! I want to catch up. It's been so long."

"She'll be there," GG said.

I shot him a dirty look. He continued. "You need to get out of the house and make some friends."

Fia laughed. "Please?"

"Okay. Okay. I'll come!"

"Great," Fia said. "I'll jot my address down for you when we're done."

****

By the time we left the clinic, it was almost lunch time. GG and I celebrated his newfound freedom by getting his favorite drive-thru and eating it in the truck at the wayside rest. It was something we did as a special treat when I was little after dentist appointments or getting a booster shot at the clinic. Why GG made us eat in the truck was never something I questioned, but now I asked him. "What's wrong with eating inside the restaurant?"

"Too crowded. Besides, this view is much nicer, wouldn't you say?"

"Sure." The wayside rest was a lookout spot with a wide view of the river and the high train bridge that ran over it just a bit in the distance. It was an old wooden trestle, one of the last in the area, according to GG. He usually made us wait at the lookout until a train crossed before we could leave. "But you just made fun of me for being socially inept at the clinic, and I'm starting to realize where I got it from, or rather who I got it from."

"Can't a man enjoy nature in peace?" he said, proving my point.

I shook my head and we ate in silence. Just as we were finishing up, I heard a train horn blast in the distance. Not a minute later, it was chugging across the bridge. We watched it until it was gone, then GG said, "Okay. Let's go."

I smiled and started the truck.

The second we got home, GG hobbled off with his cane heading toward the barn. "You need to come back in an hour or I'll send out a search party," I hollered at his backside.

"Will do, Lu!"

Inside, I sat down at my mother's desk and tried to get some work done. Instead, I found myself continually going back to the online photo of Jeffrey Donovan as if staring at it long enough would explain everything and suddenly make sense to me. I'd also been able to learn that he'd apparently only done four years in prison, which I found to be horrifying. He took my twin, my best friend, away from me, and he was able to continue to pursue his own life after he was released just a few years later. It felt so unfair. The fact that he was also an artist still sat strangely in my brain. Was that just a strange coincidence? And why was it when I looked at him, I got an uneasy feeling. I guess it was simply because I was looking into the eyes of a cold-blooded killer. I could almost understand why my mother had kept it from me.

I had nobody to talk to about it. My first instinct was to tell Brad what I'd learned, but I couldn't. I'd gone over and over it, especially after talking with Max, but I'd come to the conclusion that I'd blown it. I was a total idiot and I was mortified and embarrassed about how I'd acted the other night. The best thing to do now was to leave him alone. I'd hurt him and I wanted to give him space. And I was confused. What did I want out of our relationship? All I knew at the moment was that I missed his friendship. It wasn't fair to go back to him now, no matter how much I regretted how things played out.

I couldn't help but also wonder why I still had nagging questions about Jeffrey Donovan. Something still seemed not quite right. I just couldn't figure out what. A part of me wanted to push, but the other half didn't want to tip my mother's mental progress in the wrong direction. It did seem that things were going well for her. I could see she was happy, and while I could be bitter about that, I was trying to be more mature than I had been with her previously. I decided for now it was best to resign myself to the fact that this was just how things were going to be. I wasn't going to know any more about my past than I currently did. I was fooling myself though, because I knew I was never going to be okay with it.

Chapter Twenty-Two

It did not surprise me that Fia's house was an absolutely stunning, remodeled Victorian in a quaint little neighborhood in Marina just outside of Saltwater. Pulling up, I was intimidated by the very expensive, sleek-looking cars in the parking lot. I was too old to be embarrassed by material things, but I may have subconsciously shot past the house and parked GG's old pick-up down the road a bit. He'd kept the Old Girl in good shape, and it fit in just fine on the farm, but it definitely stood out in this upscale neighborhood.

Fia greeted me warmly. She wore a great looking coral wrap dress that went surprisingly well with her orange hair. I would never have thought to pair the two colors together, but I wasn't much for fashion. I'd agonized over my own outfit, but I hadn't packed a lot of nice clothes and I ultimately went with the basic black top and jeans. I had at least fixed my hair and put on some nice earrings and lipstick. I tended to stick with comfort over style, which again, went just fine on a farm, not so much at a dinner party with people I did not know.

I handed her the flowers and bottle of wine I'd picked up on the way. I'd learned from my previous mistakes. This time, I'd given myself more time and had ended up being early.

"Come on in," she said. "I'm so glad your grandpa forced you to come."

We laughed as she set the gifts down on a table in the foyer and gave me a tour of the house before stopping at a large playroom full of scattered toys to introduce me to her three children. They were accompanied by a babysitter who I assumed to be a live-in nanny.

"Guys? Hello? Come meet Luna." They stopped playing and marched over and stood facing us. "This is Tad. He's four, Soph is six. And this is Claire. She's two."

"And a half," the littlest one said. She was dressed in a sparkly princess gown and tiara and was the only of the three to also have red hair.

"And a half," Fia added.

"Hi," they all said in practiced unison.

"Hi!" I bent down to their level. "It's very nice to meet you."

"Luna is one of my oldest friends," Fia said. "We met in elementary school."

They nodded.

"She illustrates children's books. That means that she creates the drawings or pictures in them."

More nodding.

"That's a pretty cool job, wouldn't you say?"

More nodding, followed by some longing glances back at the toys strewn about the floor of the playroom.

"Anything you've worked on that they might know at all?" Fia asked.

"Oh. Um. Let's see…maybe *Charlie's Lost Tooth*?"

"Do we have that book?" Fia asked.

Blank stares.

"Or…*Dining with the Dinos*," I offered.

More blank stares.

"Maybe…*Hills Over Heather's House*?"

"Oh! We've read that one, haven't we, Allison?"

The nanny nodded. "The illustrations are really amazing, too."

"Thank you," I said, blushing.

"I like that book, Mommy!" Sophie yelled.

"Me, too," Tad agreed.

"That is so cool, Luna! Truly. Okay," Fia said. "You can go back to playing. Please, behave." They gave a quick wave and were off. We walked down the hall, leaving behind the sounds of giddy toddler's squealing in the background.

Fia said, "My husband is in the kitchen. It sounds like a few other guests have arrived. We'd better go see."

I followed her down the hallway lined with framed photographs of the kids and we entered the kitchen. It was a massive open kitchen/dining area. A huge spread of food lined the center of the table. Fia introduced me to her husband, Dave, and the couple who had arrived, then got us all drinks. I was worried that I would be the only single person, but then another man showed up and then I wondered if it was a set up.

His name was Johan. He was very Scandinavian looking, with blond hair and piercing blue eyes. He wore a suit coat over a white t-shirt with dark jeans. "Did you guys notice that Ford pickup down the street?" He snickered. "I haven't seen one of those since I was a kid. Very vintage chic."

I hoped nobody was looking at me because I was certain I was blushing, but this time it wasn't because I was being praised. I was glad I'd decided to park the truck away from the house, because I could tell from Johan's tone that he didn't think it was chic at all. I should not have cared, but deep down I definitely did.

I was seated next to him at the table, which was probably not a coincidence. He told me he worked in finance, then he asked me what I did for a living.

"I worked as a graphic designer at an ad firm for the last five years, but now I'm making the transition to freelance illustration work."

"Oh? What kind of illustrations?"

"Most of my work is for children's books."

"Wow. Okay. Interesting. So, you essentially color pictures for a living?" He laughed. It was over the top, boisterous, and laced with condescending undertones.

"Something like that," I said.

"Freelance, no less."

"Uh huh. Is there something wrong with freelance?"

"No. I mean, it's cool."

I thought that was going to be the end of our conversation, but he persisted. "Are you single?"

I wasn't sure I even wanted to answer the question, but I nodded.

"Kids?"

I took a sip of my drink and shook my head. Had I unintentionally signed up for a round of speed-dating? "How about you?" I asked, trying to shift the focus off of me.

"I'm recently divorced," he said.

Shocking.

"Luckily, no kids, so I really dodged a bullet there, am I right?" He laughed.

I took another drink before checking the time. How long was one round of speed dating, I wondered?

After dinner, we retired into the living room where a fire roared in a gorgeous modern marble slab fireplace with a mantel lined with even more perfect family photos. I purposely sat on the opposite side of the room from Johan and chatted with the other woman for a bit while Fia and Dave cleaned up in the kitchen.

When they joined us, Fia sat next to me. "Okay," she said with a sigh and a full glass of wine, "We can finally catch up. How have you been?"

"Not as busy as you, apparently," I said. "Three kids. And a doctor. So impressive, really. I'm so happy for you."

She laughed. "Well, you know, I was always around such a big family, I kind of missed all of the chaos. What about you?"

"What about me? My story is boring in comparison to yours."

"That's crazy. I think it's so cool that you pursued your art. You were always drawing cute little pictures. I think I even kept a few. Maybe they'll be worth something when you become a famous illustrator."

"Oh, I don't know about that."

"You've always been too humble," she said. "I've followed your work on social media and I'm in awe of your talent."

"You're a doctor! I just doodle. There's no comparison."

"Stop it. I wish I had artistic abilities. I admire people who do," Fia said.

"Well, thanks."

She nodded. "Anyway, I was curious to know if you ever ended up finding out who your dad is. I remember it being a pretty big deal to you growing up."

"No. I haven't, unfortunately. How about you?"

"Yeah. So, after I had the kids, I thought it would be nice for them to know their grandpa. Dave's dad has passed, and…while they have two grandmas who spoil them rotten, they didn't have any grandpas. So, I decided to track him down.

"But, you know what? I kinda wish I hadn't now. That's a terrible thing to say, I know. I don't know why I expected anything from a guy who didn't want a relationship with me when I was growing up. I really didn't want anything from him except for him to maybe take an interest in his grandkids, but…well, I tried to make it work, and eventually I had to face the reality that it wasn't ever going to."

"Oh, no. I'm so sorry."

"It's fine. I've made peace with it, but yeah. He's not a part of my life or my kids' lives. Probably for the best. Anyway, at least you have your grandpa. He's so dang cute, I can hardly stand it."

I laughed. "Yeah. He's pretty great. And probably just as hard to manage as three kids, so…"

"And it's so sweet that you moved back to take care of him. Has that been weird at all?"

"It's been an adjustment, but it's okay."

"Do you think you'll stay?" she asked.

"For good? No. Probably just as long as GG needs me."

She nodded.

As we continued to catch, her two-year-old, Claire, wandered in and sat down on Fia's lap. She was changed into a pair of pajamas that had unicorns on them. She jammed her little hand into Fia's soft curls and started twisting her teeny finger around a lock as we chatted. Fia looked at me and whispered, "This is how she soothes herself. Sorry."

Claire's eyes got heavy and soon she was sleeping

soundly in her mom's arms, a soft smile spread across her own freckled face. She was almost an exact miniature of Fia. I had never thought I'd wanted something like that for myself before I saw it happening in front of me, and at that moment I was very jealous of Fia and everything she had that I did not.

I didn't need the fancy house, live-in nanny, or the expensive cars, but I wouldn't mind a hallway lined with photos of cute kids, or a husband who cooked for me now and again. I didn't need to be a doctor or someone in finance, I could be happy with something simple with someone who cared about me.

I left there around nine thirty. When I got back into the truck, a new sense of companionship with the Old Girl arose. I was the pickup in the neighborhood full of sports cars and I was now ashamed that I'd been embarrassed about it. That was one take away from the evening. I knew what I didn't want. Another thing that struck me was that Fia had met her father and had regrets. That solidified my own decision to not pursue things further with regard to Ernie.

As I drove home, I had to go directly by Finley's Bar and Grill. I slowed down briefly and though the place appeared to be hopping, I was able to pick Brad's car out in the parking lot. Not expensive, but not vintage chic either. I only thought for the briefest second about stopping before I hit the gas and continued back to the farm. It wasn't a rustic cabin in the woods, but the farm was a close second. A person could stay up in those hills sheltered away from the rest of society with no trouble at all. I knew that from experience. I'd done it for many years. I thought I was over that, but maybe now that I was coming up on thirty, it wasn't such a bad place to be.

At least I had GG and the cows. It could be worse.

The farm was dark when I pulled in. GG had given me my own key so I didn't have to keep taking the spare out of the porch swing. I went upstairs and turned the hall light on so I could peek inside his bedroom and check on him like a mother would do for her child. He was snoring softly. I smiled to myself.

I went back downstairs, turned the television on, and fell asleep on the sofa.

Chapter Twenty-Three

The next few weeks ticked by slowly. I finished my work for the ad firm while GG was back to spending as much time away from the house as he could. He didn't need me for much except to call him in to eat and he was growing irritated with my constant checking up on him, asking how he felt, if everything was okay. He didn't have any more mishaps so I tried to ease up on him a little.

As I gave less and less time to caring for my grandfather, I fell into a funk and knew I needed a distraction. I decided to plant vegetables in Grammy's empty garden box. I couldn't bear seeing the plot of land sit dormant out the kitchen window any longer. It was late to get things in the ground for the growing season here which was a super short window, but I didn't care. It gave me a newfound purpose. I'd never liked being a farmer before, but I was suddenly excited to get my hands dirty. It was like I was turning into my revered grandmother.

My mother stopped by a couple of times with wedding coordinators, painters, carpenters, decorators, florists, and caterers. They walked around the property measuring things, discussing color schemes, dishware, and everything in between. She tried to include me, asking for my opinions on things, but I stayed out of the way for the most part, often retreating back to the garden to weed or water.

GG helped me find Grammy's tools, boots, and work gloves in the garage. Max rounded up the tomato cages for me one day and brought them out when he saw that they were actually growing big enough. I wasn't sure who was more shocked by this revelation. Everyone knew how often I'd run away from my tasks around this place when I was a girl, but at the same time, as an adult woman, I was realizing how much I actually knew about farming and was actually taking pleasure in seeing things grow.

And then it was time for me to return to New York to pack up my apartment. I made sure Max and my mom would be around to check up on GG, and I headed out for a week. This time it felt strange returning to my old life. It was like a lifetime had passed since I'd been there. I hardly felt like a New Yorker anymore.

While I sorted, donated, and boxed stuff up, I contemplated whether or not to contact Jeffrey Donovan. I wasn't sure why I was even considering it, but something was compelling me to know more about him, and why he did what he did. Did he have any remorse? Why us? What did he want that night? Was it really random? I wanted some type of explanation from him, an apology, but even with that, would I be able to forgive him for stealing from me? My entire life might have been different had he not done what he did. Every day I wondered what things would have been like if my sister had lived.

I was angry. All of the anger I'd been directing toward my mother had suddenly shifted to this man, this stranger. He took everything from me. He deprived me of a life in which I had a sidekick, a confidante, a best friend, and even a potential love interest. I lost my twin, my parents, and Brad. I was on the verge of thirty and I felt completely and utterly alone.

So, after I sorted all of my things out, packed them up, and scheduled shippers to come for the boxes, I had a few days left with nothing to do in an empty apartment. I took the train to Brooklyn one afternoon and I went to the art gallery that had advertised several of Jeffery Donavon's pieces currently on exhibit. I hadn't been able to get myself to message him, but I still wanted some insight into his soul and what better way to find that than through his art.

The gallery was called "Creative Space" and was housed in an old warehouse. Their primary focus was on huge installation pieces, mostly 3D sculptures, so the space was large. I looked around and didn't see anybody minding the desk. A few people were roaming about, but it was obvious they were only there to check out the art, like me. Once I was sure that nobody resembling the man I'd seen pictures of online was here, I went in search of Jeffrey's artwork.

I found the metal sculptures and stopped to take them in. They weren't very different from the other pieces I'd seen photographs of on his website. Large hunks of twisted alloys were mashed together with jagged, rough edges glued with visible welds. They were sort of ugly and crude. The overall products were of nondescript shapes attached to wooden bases. I walked around them, viewing them from various angles, trying to understand their deeper meaning, to connect to them in some way, but like the material they were made from, they exuded an ugly and confused vibe and left me cold. If the person who created this was anything like the piece, I wanted nothing to do with him. I wasn't sure why I would have expected anything else.

I shuddered and walked out. Much like with Ernie, seeing these pieces only strengthened my decision not to contact Jeffrey Donovan. Maybe I would someday, but for now, this visit offered the closure I was seeking. I was ready to get back to Alton and try to move on from everything.

I spent my last few days in New York cleaning out my apartment, doing some chores, and I stopped into my old office to say goodbye and retrieve the few personal items I had in my desk. On my final night in town, I had drinks with a couple of colleagues and friends.

By the time I got back on a plane to return to Alton, my mood had shifted somewhat. I was surprised to find that I was actually itching to return to the farm. I no longer harbored the same negative feelings toward my mother I had before, and if anything, I was ready to start trying to forge something new with her. I missed GG and worried about him when I wasn't there to keep an eye on him. So, I returned feeling renewed and knowing without a doubt that being in Alton was the best thing for me right now.

It helped that it was finally warm enough to feel like summer had arrived. My mom was supposed to pick me up from the airport, but Ernie arrived in her place. While this shouldn't have shocked me, sometimes my mother never ceased to amaze me.

We drove with the windows down. It was too loud to speak much over the thirty minutes we were in the car. I was no longer angry with him, but I still didn't have to like him no matter who he was to me. Father by marriage or blood? I still had no idea. And the fact that I was still unsure of the nature of our biological relationship was potentially at the heart of my discomfort with him.

He made it hard for me to dislike him though. When we arrived back at the farm, he helped me with my heavy luggage. Stepping out of the car, the air smelled cleaner, less like wet manure, birds were chirping, the grass was finally greening, and the sun was actually hot on my skin for the first time. I'd forgotten how it took until late June for summer to take hold in Minnesota.

The farm started buzzing with excitement because the wedding was taking place in a few short days. I heard echoes of pounding from somewhere near the pole barn, tables and chairs and other things were stacked up in places, and people were unloading bins of what looked like decorations from their cars. The biggest change was that the house and porch, including the swing, had fresh coats of paint. I'd only been gone a week, but it was like I'd returned to someplace else entirely.

"Wow," I said to Ernie as we unloaded my stuff from his trunk, "I thought Mom said you were going to have something simple and small?"

He guffawed. "I wish I had gotten that in writing."

"It's getting real, huh?"

"I'll say."

"Are you getting nervous?"

"Me? No. If anything, your mom will be the one who changes her mind."

"Stop it," I said. "Not with all of the planning she's done."

GG came out to greet us. I gave him a hug. "Looks like a damn circus is coming to town, eh?" he said.

"I'll say. Did she invite all of Alton?"

"I wouldn't put it past her."

Ernie insisted on taking the majority of my bags inside. He even carried them up the stairs for me. When he set the last one down, I thanked him for the ride and help with the luggage and expected him to rush off to help my mother, but he stood awkwardly for a second looking at me. Then he cleared his throat and said, "Can I talk to you about something?"

My chest constricted a bit. I thought this might be it, the moment he told me he was my biological father. "Sure," I said. I wasn't sure which one of us now seemed more nervous. I sat down on the bed in an attempt to ward off a possible panic attack.

He dug his right hand into his pocket. "I hope you aren't still angry with me about our last conversation."

"No. It's water under the bridge. Besides, you might have been right about a few things."

"I'm glad. Marrying your mother…well, that makes us family and that's special. It's a big deal to me. So, if you'll let me, I'd like to be a part of your life." He pulled his hand out of his pocket and handed me a small, wrapped box. "I got you a little something. You don't have to open it right now."

I wasn't expecting it, but the gesture was so sweet and genuine, I almost teared up. "Thank you," I said. "My mom seems very happy, so I guess that makes me happy for you both."

Ernie smiled. "I better go tackle this list before she gets unhappy with me."

"Good luck with that."

After he left, I set the gift from Ernie on the dresser and started to unpack my luggage. One of the bags I had was full of office supplies, so I went into my mother's bedroom to set it in there. I couldn't help but notice an incredibly gorgeous, cream-colored wedding dress hanging in the open closet. I went over to it and simply gawked for a second without touching it.

Suddenly, she was standing behind me. "Do you like it?"

I turned to her. "It's beautiful."

"Is it too much? I have this other plum colored dress," she said, moving a few of the items around in the closet to reveal the second dress.

"No. The white one is perfect."

"Are you sure?" She pulled away from the closet and stood wringing her hands together.

"You doing okay? It's a lot, huh?"

"Yeah. I don't know what I was thinking. I'm a middle-aged woman. What am I doing?"

"Hey." I took her hands. "It's going to be okay. Ernie is a great guy."

"I just…"

"Mom, look at me. Take some deep breaths."

She did.

"You got this. The wedding is just the performance that happens. The marriage is the real thing. You and Ernie have already essentially been living like a marriage couple and it's going great, right?"

"Yes."

"So don't worry about the wedding. Think of it as a party to celebrate the thing that you already know you can do. Okay?"

She nodded. "Okay. That…makes sense."

"Good. Feel better?"

"Yes."

"Now, what can I do? Do you have a chore list for me? I'm ready to help."

My mother smiled. "That would be wonderful. I have a million things for you to do."

Chapter Twenty-Four

The morning of the wedding started out gray and overcast, and it appeared there was a chance of rain even though the forecast hadn't hinted at it. My mother fretted, pacing around the house, while I helped GG into what he kept calling his monkey suit. It was a little tricky to get the pants Mom bought for him over his cast, but we managed. He wanted to wear his work boot on his good foot, but Mom put her own boot down on that idea. I dug deep into the back of his closet, found a pair of black leather dress shoes, polished the left one up, and laced it on his foot while he muttered under his breath.

Once he was taken care of, I showered and sat on my bed in my robe with Ernie's gift. I opened the box to find a lovely teardrop pearl necklace that would pair perfectly with the dress I planned to wear for the wedding, so I found my mother in her bedroom standing in her robe with her arms crossed and asked if she'd help clasp it on for me.

"Ernie gave you this?"

"Yes. It was very sweet."

"It looks great," she said. She sat down on her bed and furrowed her brow.

"How are you holding up? Are you feeling okay?"

"Yes. Just waiting for the hair and makeup people to arrive."

"Okay. I'm going to go finish getting dressed. Call

me if you need anything."

She nodded.

I had been trying to keep out of the way of the circus since I'd returned, unless called upon to help out, but for the most part, I'd managed to avoid seeing the finished product until the day of the wedding. After I was dressed, and Mom was stuck with her hair being done, she asked me to check on things in the barn to see if anybody needed anything. I said I would.

I made my way out to the pole barn, which sat behind the red barn down on the backside of the hill. The pole barn was a big hangar essentially, used to store the farm equipment. It had always been a bit of an eyesore, the inner workings of a farm, essentially, and not the pretty ones but the guts, the dirty, greasy insides.

So when I got near and saw what it had been transformed into, I was floored. It had been painted with a fresh coat of dark brown stain throughout. The hangar doors were wide open, and from the rafters hung at least a hundred sets of white string lights. Gauzy white tulle wrapped the thick beams that held up the barn's structure. I'd never seen the floor looking as immaculate as it did now. Where were the giant grease spots left from the tractors? And where had they moved all of that equipment? In its place, at least a dozen round tables had been evenly spaced. Each had been dressed in white linens and full place settings. Off to the side of the barn, beneath a large stretch of clean white canvas, chairs were being set up facing a faux-rustic podium that looked like it had been handcrafted specifically for the occasion. It looked amazing. Very rustic chic. And not in the ironic way that Johan had used to goof on the truck. This was the good kind. I checked in with the various people running around setting things up asking if they needed anything, but everyone seemed on task. Things were running smoothly.

As I started back to the house, I saw Max pull up and park not in his usual place, but in a spot that had been sectioned off for the guests to park. He was dressed in a suit and didn't have his cowboy hat on. A woman, who I assumed was Sherry, got out of the passenger seat. And then a third person got out of the backseat. Someone I wasn't expecting to see. Brad.

For some reason, I hadn't considered that he would be invited. Of course, I knew that Max and his wife would be here, but Brad? Never mind being invited, the fact that he showed was surprising, especially given his very non-existent relationship with my mother. All I could think was that he was here for his dad's sake. I respected that.

I managed to avoid contact with them by dodging into the cow barn. I wandered through and headed back to the house trying to figure out how I was going to get through this without a panic attack. I already felt my pulse quickening. Luckily, I was so busy with random chores, I didn't have much time to think more about it until the wedding itself was underway.

By the time the ceremony started, the clouds lifted and turned the day nearly perfect—sunny and seventy-five degrees. An overwhelming scent of lilac and honeysuckle wafted in the air, and I couldn't help but question who my mother had hired to remove the normal farm smell of cow manure and pesticides for her special day.

The actual nuptials were short and sweet, and I'd managed to avoid Brad up until then thanks to my mother inviting the entire town, though I could see him seated at the end of the row of chairs to my left as I sat down. Looking around, I had no idea who most of the guests were, though there were definitely plenty of them. It seemed like most of the members of the Alton Upper Valley Fire and Rescue were in attendance and I recognized a few old friends of the family, my mother's boss, and several of Ernie's family members whom I'd been introduced to as things were getting started.

GG bounced his good leg in his seat and rolled his eyes at me a few times during the ceremony like a small child and I had to hold back from giggling. It was a good thing it was short because the old man was getting antsy. I should have brought him a juice box and some goldfish crackers to distract him.

After they exchanged vows, which were surprisingly traditional, my mom and Ernie kissed, and when the officiant pronounced them, "Ernest and Jennifer Schmitt," the new couple walked back to the house while everyone threw corn kernels at them. According to the printed card sitting on my chair, there was to be a cocktail hour before the dinner reception in the pole barn.

I got stuck in a conversation with someone who introduced themselves as a second cousin of Aunt Betty. I had no idea who that was, but I chatted politely with her as I watched Brad wander away out of the corner of my eye. Once I was able to break free from the crowd, I hiked up the hill.

When I got there, Brad was sitting in our secret spot. I plopped down beside him. "Thought I might find you here," I said.

He glanced at me before redirecting his gaze back

down the valley. "You look nice."

I bit my lip and said, "Now that I have you cornered, I wondered if we could talk?"

"Okay."

"I'm sorry about how things ended. I was an idiot. I assumed you'd never want to speak to me again, and frankly, I wouldn't blame you if that's still the case, but—"

"I never said I didn't want to see you again. That was all you."

"Right. I know. I think it was just my defense, but I thought I was leaving…"

"But now you're staying?"

"Yeah. I'm staying. Either way, I'm really, really sorry. And…I've made an appointment to get a DNA test, so…if you care to join me…"

He gave me a devilish grin. "Maybe the curse is finally broken?"

"Or maybe we're cousins," I reminded him.

"Right, but we might not be."

"That's true," I said.

"Either way, I'm glad you're staying."

"Does that mean we're good?"

"We've always been good," he said. "But…"

"Uh oh. But what?"

He turned to me. "If we do this test and say, hypothetically speaking, we find out Mickey isn't your dad, then what exactly happens, all jokes aside? Because…I think you know my feelings toward you, but I'm a little less clear on what yours are."

"Well, let's just say that, hypothetically, if I was certain that you weren't my cousin and you happened to try to kiss me again sometime, like you did when we were sixteen in this very spot, I might just let you."

"Really?" he said. "And not just because you've had a little too much to drink?"

"Oh, God. Did I? I don't even remember…"

He smiled. "You did."

"Did I mention that I am so, so sorry?"

"You did. I wish you didn't have to be…"

"Maybe next time…" I smiled and stood up. "I better get back to the party. I'm supposed to be in charge of something or other. You coming?"

"Sure."

Chapter Twenty-Five

The string lights glowed with a magical effect as the daylight faded and everyone started to gather for dinner. A light evening breeze kept the temperature in the old barn from getting too stuffy. It was nice. I only wished Grammy were here to be a part of it all, but other than that, I was glad the day had turned out so well for my mom and Ernie.

I did the tasks Mom had assigned me, and I even mingled a little with a few people while Brad got us some drinks. The DJ started to play some music and then he made an announcement that dinner would be served, and people should find their seat assignments.

I was seated at a table next to Ernie's sister, Bethany, on my left. And to the right of me was Brad. It was a good thing we'd made up or it could have been a very long and awkward dinner. I was a little surprised my mom placed us next to one another since she didn't seem to like him, but as it was, I was happy to have someone to talk to that I knew. I'd already made enough small talk with strangers for one day.

GG was sitting on the other side of Brad, and next to him was Ernie's mother, Martha. The barn was growing louder with so many people talking and the music from the D.J. bouncing off the walls, so I couldn't hear what they were saying, but I was amused watching Martha try to navigate a conversation with GG. He acted more interested in the plate of food the server had set in front of him than he was talking to a single, old lady. It was clear he'd rather be sitting alone on the porch with his newspaper.

I introduced myself to Bethany and checked out her facial features, trying to see what Diana Butcher saw that we shared in common. Her hair was platinum blonde but also so obviously dyed that it still didn't help me much. She was short but also not as fit as her brother. In fact, she was quite the opposite. She was pleasant enough, and we made small talk for a bit while we ate our salads. As we waited for the servers to bring around the second course, I got bold and said to her, "You know, it's funny. I ran into Diana Butcher the other week and she said that she thought the two of us look alike. That's sort of weird, right?"

"What?" she asked through the noise.

I repeated myself. "She said we could be related," I added.

She looked at me hard for a second. "Why would she say that, I wonder?"

"Maybe it had something to do with Ernie and my mom going to prom together," I said with a light laugh.

She did not return the laugh or look amused in the least, but I pushed ahead. "I mean…I don't know who my father is, so…maybe? It could be Ernie for all we know."

"Ernie? No! Your dad is Mickey Finley."

Hearing his name, Brad leaned toward me trying to hear what we were discussing.

"What?" I said, thinking maybe I hadn't heard her right through the noise. "No."

"Yeah." She nodded with vigor.

"I don't…"

"Ernie had the biggest crush on your mom in high school, but she was madly in love with Mickey. The whole school knew it. Her parents forbid her from seeing him though, so when Ernie asked her to the dance, she said yes. I was mad because I figured she was just using my brother, and I was proved right when I saw her and Mickey take off on his motorcycle the first chance they got that night. It broke my brother's heart, but I guess it all worked out in the end."

"Well, sure," I said. "But my mother went to college shortly after that, so my dad could be someone she met in school."

She shrugged, taking a sip of her drink. "Sure, but when Jenny left for school, Mickey became mysteriously absent from Alton. Rumors were flying that they were still together."

"Rumors don't prove anything," I said, defiantly.

"No, but my ex was friends with Mick and they stayed in touch. Mickey came through every now and again over the years on his trucking route and they'd meet up for a beer every so often. He confirmed that the rumors were true."

I got up, feeling dizzy. "Excuse me, I need to…" I started walking away from the table.

"Luna?" Brad called.

"I just need a little air. I'll be right back."

I fought my way out of the barn and tried to stay calm as there were still pockets of people gathered outside. I just needed to get away, so I started walking, unsure of where I was headed. This couldn't be happening. Not now. I couldn't even get close enough to my mother to talk to her even if I'd wanted to. She'd been swarmed by people since she and Ernie entered the pole barn. This was certainly not the time or the place to have this discussion. The problem was, they were leaving for their honeymoon right after the party. If I didn't get answers tonight, I would have to wait until they got back in a week.

I continued on, directionless, almost at a sprint now, trying to sort things out in my head. It was dark and the air felt sticky and sweat poured from me, but I thought it was just because of how sick I felt. It turned out to be because the rain that had threatened to come down this morning was now ready to come down. A bolt of lightning lit up everything around me, and I saw that I was near the red shed at the edge of the property. Just as the deluge began to soak through my dress, I ran into the shed for shelter.

As soon as I caught my breath, I took my phone out and turned the flashlight on and looked around. It took me a second to realize that I was finally in the red shed, the space I'd been barred from as a child, the place where I didn't believe my mother had created art, but now knew that was actually possible, so it didn't surprise me to see some canvases stacked up on the floor in the corner. They were face down. I picked up the first one and turned it around expecting to see a pretty landscape such as the one that had been hanging in the gallery in Saltwater.

But that wasn't at all what I saw. I dropped the canvas and stumbled back, trying to get away from the scene. The painting seemed to have other plans, as it landed upright. My foot caught on the uneven floor as I moved away from the horror in front of me, and I fell to the ground on my butt, dropping my phone beside me, snuffing out the light.

My pulse quickened and my vision blurred. And suddenly everything started to piece itself together. The images on the canvas melded with the blank spaces in my brain because I was there that night, just on the edge of it. I was four years old again standing in our apartment in Minneapolis with Grammy's crocheted afghan draped over my head in fear of the yelling happening in the living room. I'd gotten up out of bed when Sonny had, but I stayed back and watched it all unfold, peeking out between the gaps in the blanket over my face. I could see it now in my own head just as it was painted onto the canvas before me. A shadowy figure is near the front door of the apartment. And then a loud bang.

Dark red paint splattered the entire canvas as if Jackson Pollock had murdered someone. But just below the surface of it, I saw the silhouetted man plainly on the canvas. In my own mind, the figure materialized into a real person. I fully expected it to be someone resembling the person I now knew as Jeff Donovan, but it wasn't. Instead his face was covered in dark facial hair. A blue and white bandana was wrapped around his forehead. He was Mickey Finley.

My stomach lurched. I picked up my phone and was ready to run, but I couldn't. I had to make myself see more, to understand. I shined the light on the other paintings, determined to get answers. I flipped through them all, looking through the splattered red paint drips to the picture behind, but they were all relatively the same, dozens of them showing the crime scene, the scene I could now see with my own mind. I'd been there.

Then I found some toward the bottom of the stack that were different. Though they were also doused in a top layer of thick red paint, these paintings showed a young boy lying on the ground next to a large piece of farming machinery. This must have been Robbie, my mom's brother, the one who was killed by the combine. I hadn't even considered the similarities until now, seeing the red paint sprayed over the top of both scenes side-by-side.

A gentle knock came from the half open door of the red shed, and I looked up to see Brad standing there. "Hey. Are you okay?"

I wiped my face, realizing it was wet not only from the rain, but from tears. "How'd you know I was out here?"

"I saw your flashlight." He took a tentative step in. "What happened back there? I could only hear part of it."

"I finally know what's been triggering my panic attacks."

"Really? What?"

"Mickey Finley."

"Huh?"

"I must have seen the whole thing, my sister being killed, but I blocked it out."

"What does Mickey have to do with it?"

I held up the painting for him to see. "He was there."

"Why?"

"I don't know, but according to Bethany, it's because he's my father."

He sat down next to me. "What?"

"She said she and her ex-husband were friends with him, that he's stopped in Alton a few times over the years when he was driving his trucking route. He'd confirmed the rumor."

"I mean…"

"No. It makes sense. I found this newspaper clipping

in my mother's desk a few weeks ago. It was a police blot of the night Sonny died. It said a man named Jeffrey Donovan was charged with the crime. I brought it to my mom and asked if he was my dad. She said he was the man breaking in, but I knew deep down as she was explaining it all to me that something didn't add up, I just couldn't put my finger on it.

"Because the news clipping indicated there had been an argument. I had no memory of Mickey being there, but he clearly had been fighting with this other man. What about? I don't know. But it somehow led to my sister being killed. And if Mickey isn't my father, what would he have been doing there? Not only that, but the reporter also mentioned something about a possible link to a biker gang. This Jeffrey guy, I found out, isn't a biker, he's a modern sculptor. I think the reporter confused the two." Anger poured back into me. "I'm so frustrated. It's like I'm back to square one again." I looked at him.

"Your mom obviously has more explaining to do," he said.

"Yeah, but now I'm going to have to wait until after she returns from her honeymoon to ask her. God! I should have known not to trust my mother. She was obviously lying."

"Why would she lie? Why not just tell you Mickey is your dad?"

I looked at him. "And if he is, it's like *we're* back to square one again. I'm so sorry."

"It's not your fault. We'll get it worked out."

"Yeah, but not until after the honeymoon."

"Well, we've waited ten years, what's another week?"

Chapter Twenty-Six

The last thing I wanted to do was go back to that barn and continue the evening like nothing had changed, because everything had changed. I'd unlocked the piece of my brain that had been shielding me from seeing my twin sister's death. It was strange to have a memory that was essentially new, but this one was also terrifying and grizzly, and I wanted to shove it back into the blackness, but it didn't work that way. And now I had to go back to the party and act like I was having a good time and happy for my mom.

I wasn't sure anymore why I was even willing to give that satisfaction to my mother. She'd obviously lied to me and now I was more confused than I'd ever felt. As Brad and I walked back, the rain had abated, leaving behind cool air and a wet ground. I slipped my heels off and held them in one hand while also holding the bottom of my dress up, so it didn't get any wetter than it already was. We took our time, neither of us anxious to return to the party. I was shivering, and Brad stopped to put his suit coat around my shoulders.

As we slowly trudged through the tall grass, I sniffled. Brad asked if I was okay. He reached for my hand, but thought better of it.

"Now that I remember, it keeps playing over and over again in my head. And all of those paintings...I almost feel bad for my mother now, having to witness two tragic events like that. And yet, I'm furious with her for continuing to play games with me. What is she hiding? Why does she keep lying to me?"

"I don't know," he said. "But I still think there's a chance that Bethany is wrong."

"Only because you want her to be," I teased.

"Well, yes. But also…a rumor doesn't prove anything. You know what high school rumors are like."

"Uh, no, actually. I don't."

"Oh, that's right. Well, for example then…in sixth grade Arthur Morton started a rumor that my mom had faked her death because she wanted to start a new, better family."

"God. That's awful."

"It is, but it happened so often, most kids figured out pretty quickly it was made up nonsense. A few, however, thrived off of fueling the rumor flames, and Bethany seems like she might be one of those types. I saw her eyes when she was talking to you, even though I couldn't hear what she was saying. She was really enjoying herself."

"You could be right. It sounded like she still harbors some resentment toward my mom for breaking Ernie's heart back in high school."

"And this was how she was going to get back at her," he said.

"That's twisted."

"It is. But that's not the only reason why I don't believe it. Because, again, when we were looking at those old photos of you and your sister…I just don't see any resemblance between you and Mickey, but I did see some in Sonny. It's still strange to me that you two looked nothing alike."

"Like day and night, right?" I said with a dry laugh. "Get it? Sun and the Moon?"

"Is that why Jenny named you that? Because you didn't look alike? Or..." He grabbed my arm and we both stopped in our tracks. "Luna...is it possible that you and Sonny aren't twins?"

"What? No!"

"Think about it. Maybe Micky was there that night because Sonny was his kid?"

"It would make sense, except that Sonny and I have the same birth date. We have to be twins."

"Unless your mom lied about that too," he said.

"True. I guess anything's possible at this point. She's clearly hiding something."

We started walking again. When we got close to the barn, I stopped. "I can't believe I have to go in there now and pretend everything's fine. I really don't know what to say to Bethany Schmitt either."

"I know. We can trade places if that would help at all?"

"It would. Thanks."

"It's no problem. I deal with people like her at the bar all the time."

We stood facing one another in the moonlight. I wanted so badly to kiss him again, but now I couldn't. The whole thing was such a mess, I just wanted to curl up into a ball and cry myself to sleep. Instead, I had to go back to a party where people were going to want to dance and talk and have a good time. "How long do you think I have to stay for and not look like a total jerk?" I asked him.

"Hmm. Maybe another hour or so? You can probably sneak out undetected after they've cut the cake.

By then people will be dancing and the drinks will be flowing."

I took a deep breath. "Okay. Better get it over with."

Brad nodded.

"Hey," I said. "I want you to know that whatever happens, I don't want that to come between us again. I've really missed you, Bradley Finley. So, if we find out that Mickey is my dad, can we at least remain friends?"

"No," he said.

My heart dropped. "What? Why not?"

"We can't be friends…because we'll be cousins, which is even better," he said with a smirk. "Just think about it. You'll be a Finley. You can come and work with me and Kelsey at the bar."

"Oh my God!" I gave him a playful push. "Luna Finley? That doesn't sound right at all."

"I think it sounds pretty good actually, I mean, maybe in another circumstance."

This time I smirked.

"Hey…got you to smile," he said.

I smacked him lightly on the shoulder, gave him his coat back, and we entered the barn.

We took our new seats. A porterhouse steak was plated in front of me and a roasted chicken breast was in Brad's place. We picked up our plates and swapped them without a word.

GG was cutting up his steak, still trying to avoid eye contact with Ernie's mom. "Everything okay?" he asked me. "You're soaked to the bone."

"Everything's fine."

"How long do I have to stay?" he asked.

I almost snorted. "Another hour?"

"What?" he yelled over the noise.

"An hour."

He checked his wrist watch. "A half hour?"

"Sure." I realized GG was my ticket out. "I'll walk you back in half an hour, okay?"

"Sounds like a good plan to me."

As we started to eat, Ernie's best friend, Doug, got up to make a toast. He was a fellow paramedic and he rambled on for a long time about how great it was to work alongside Ernie saving people's lives each and every day. I was starting to feel slightly bad about my mother, thinking nobody would stand and gush about her like that and wondering if I was supposed to, but also knowing that there was no way I could ever do such a thing. But then the woman I'd met at the art gallery stood and talked about how my mother had changed her life, had shown her how to express herself through art, and on and on. Part of me was relieved that my mom wasn't humiliated and part of me was angry all over again for not knowing this side of her. Would these competing emotions about my mother ever leave me? It didn't seem like it.

Luckily, it wasn't long after that that Mom and Ernie cut the cake and GG stared at me across the table like a dog waiting to be taken out to use the restroom. I said goodnight to Brad, and GG and I worked our way through the crowd, only stopping once to chat with an old neighbor, another farmer who'd sold his land across the street a few years ago and moved to the senior living facility down by the water. He told GG it was the best decision he'd ever made. GG scoffed at the notion, telling Fred he'd rather die than live anywhere besides this piece of property. I realized he likely would die right here, in the exact place he'd been born, and that was what he wanted. That was the goal. That was GG.

Once we were outside the barn and the noise subsided, I said to my grandpa, "I went into the red shed."

He didn't stop hobbling along, but he glanced at me with a startled look on his face. "So…you saw them then? Those…paintings?"

"I did."

"Now you know why I tried to keep you from that place all this time."

When we reached the porch, GG sat down on his chair. I sat on the swing next to him. I saw him close his eyes in the glow of the porch light. I thought he'd dozed off, but then he said, "We didn't always know how to handle Jenny. It was hard on everybody, but we didn't always understand what was going on with your mom. When she started to make those paintings, well, we thought maybe it would help her, so I built the red shed and put the lock on it to keep you away. I'm not sure if we always did the right thing. When you become a parent, you'll see. It's not always easy. It's usually not easy. You though, Lu, you were the easy part. That isn't what I'm trying to say here."

"I understand. You know, a part of me always thought that Mom was making up her issues, like it was all an act, a way to get attention. I think that was partly why I resented her so much. But seeing those paintings, I think I was completely wrong."

"Nobody is right or wrong. That's the hardest part about it. What happened was terrible. No two buts about it," GG said.

"Now I understand why you and Grammy always made so many concessions for her. It was hard for me to do that."

"You didn't know. We thought at the time that shielding you from it was the best solution. You were just a little girl. Maybe we were wrong."

"No. I think you were right. I wouldn't have been able to process it back then."

GG nodded. "I wish things had been different, but we tried our best."

"I know." We sat for a minute enjoying the silence. "You want me to get your pipe and newspaper?"

"If you don't mind."

I went in and retrieved GG's things. I found his house slippers, too. When I brought one back, I handed him the pipe and paper and slipped off his one tight dress shoes. As I put his slipper on, he said, "I want you to know, Lu…your grandma and me…we've always been proud of you."

I got up and kissed his forehead. "I know and I love you."

I went inside and threw myself onto my bed. I wasn't sure how it was all going to end, but GG was right. Everyone did the best they could with the circumstances. While we couldn't change those things, maybe we could fix some going forward.

Chapter Twenty-Seven

The next morning, I couldn't force myself to get up even though the twin bed from my youth was uncomfortable. Not only did I not want to face the day, but I was still tired from lying awake listening to the distant sounds of music, laughing, and celebration coming from the barn, trying to blot out the new memory I'd been given back.

I was still awake to hear Mom and Ernie drive off in the 1950 Chevy Ernie had rented for their getaway. They were headed to a remote cabin in the Northwoods where they wouldn't have phone service, so even if I had wanted to talk to my mom, I wouldn't have been able to do it.

It was going to be a long week of waiting to get to the bottom of things. In my restless state, I'd also pondered something Brad said, where he'd speculated about me and Sonny not being twins. Was it possible? It would have certainly answered some of the questions. I shot up in bed realizing there was a way to find out without waiting for my mom to return to civilization, or at least the farm, in a week.

As I put my robe on, I headed across the hall and into my mother's bedroom. I frantically pulled out all of the drawers in the side of the roll top desk, searching, but they were empty. Then I opened her closet and dug around in a few cardboard boxes she'd left behind, but they only contained old clothes. Her dresser had been cleared out, too.

I put on a pair of sweats and a t-shirt and went downstairs. I searched in every nook and cranny of the den, which also doubled as Grammy's sewing room. She had an old utility table set up against the wall that she called her crafting table, but she did everything there, including all of the paperwork that kept the farm afloat. GG wasn't good with numbers, according to him, and Grammy was the educated one, so she handled all the bills and kept the files in order.

Her sewing machine was still plugged in, and on the floor beside the table was a stack of quilting fabric, a basket of yarn, and a locked file cabinet which housed all of the important family documents. GG had given me the keys after she died and I'd been taking care of the monthly bills since then. Grammy had given me my birth certificate before I moved to New York, but I'd never actually seen Sonny's. It had to be here somewhere.

I spent an hour or so shifting through the files. Everything was in there, everything except a copy of Sonny's birth certificate.

Not sure where else to look, I gave up and started making a late breakfast. I figured I'd lure GG back inside with some eggs and bacon and ask him if he had any idea where my sister's birth certificate might be filed away. While I stood buttering GG's toast from behind the butcher block table, I had a clear shot from the kitchen into the dining area. My eyes searched beyond the oak table and stopped on the bookcase. I couldn't imagine why a birth certificate would be on the reference shelf next to the dictionary and encyclopedias, but I'd checked everywhere else.

I was about to head toward it when I smelled something burning. The bacon. I whipped around, turned the heat off the burner, grabbed the tongs, and plunked the blackened pork from the pan as smoke filled the kitchen, but I was far too late. The fire alarm started blasting a piercing warning. I grabbed the hand towel and waved it around in the air trying to dissipate the smoke. The alarm was overhead, too high for me to reach and turn off without a step stool.

I searched in the broom closet looking for the ladder, while the alarm continued screaming in my ears, but it wasn't there. When I closed the door, Max and GG were coming in the backdoor.

"I burned the bacon," I said. "I can't find the step ladder. It must have been used for the party or something."

"I'll go get one from the garage," Max said, running off.

While he did that, I threw open the few windows nearby. GG stood unphased, picking at the charred bacon on the plate. Within a minute, Max was back, ladder in hand. He climbed up and deactivated the smoke detector.

"Thank you," I said. "Do you want some breakfast? I didn't burn the eggs or the toast."

"I already ate," he said with a chuckle. "But I appreciate the offer."

"At least let me refill your coffee to take back out with you."

"That I will take."

As I poured it, I said, "I can't believe you're back here this early. What time did you leave the party last night?"

"Oh, we stayed until maybe eleven," he said. "I

noticed you two made haste pretty early."

I handed him the mug. "Yeah. It was too loud for GG in there and I'm not much of a dancer, so…"

"Understood. Okay, I'm off. Thanks for the coffee, Luna."

"Thank you for the ladder."

By the time GG and I sat down to eat, I'd completely forgotten to check the reference shelf. Between sips of coffee, I asked him if he knew where the document could be.

"What do you want with that now?"

That was a good question, one I had been unprepared to answer. I didn't want to get him all twisted up in my drama, so I just said, "I was just curious about where it might be now that Grammy isn't here to keep track of it. I haven't seen it in the file cabinet."

"Huh. If it's not in the file cabinet, then I don't know where it could be. Wait…you know what, I wonder…your Mom put a stack of boxes out in the garage while she was clearing things from her room. I suppose it could be in with that stuff."

"Oh! You might be right. I remember seeing them when Max helped me carry the desk in."

I finished eating, cleared the plates, and headed to the garage. Max was in there fixing something or other when I walked in. I said hello and started digging through Mom's boxes. I was honestly a little scared about what else I might find inside of them since I now knew her frame of mind, but I also wondered if there could be things in this pile of leftover junk somewhere, something that might unlock more answers without having to confront her again. I left no stone unturned.

My head was buried inside a box of papers when

Max came over with his coffee in hand and hovered. "Whatcha looking for?"

"Oh, uh, just something I made when I was little." I hated lying to Max, who was like an uncle to me. In fact, he might have actually been my uncle for all I knew.

He nodded and was about to walk away when my guilt got the better of me. I was not my mother. So, I said, "Actually, I'm looking for Sonny's birth certificate."

"As long as we're being honest with each other," he said, "Brad told me. On the drive home last night."

I pulled my head from the box and looked at him.

"Oh," I said, feeling oddly naked.

"I want you to know that I was being truthful with you the other night. I knew your mom and Mickey were an item back then, but beyond that...I can't say for sure. He and I weren't that close. I wish that weren't the case, but I'm afraid it is."

"GG and Gram apparently forbid my mother from seeing him. What was wrong with him?"

"Mick was the middle kid. He was always vying for attention and then he just got really rebellious. He had some problems with anger. I felt for him, I really did. He wasn't a black sheep. He projected that onto himself. Nobody was judging him, except him. He dealt with it by drinking. He was so fixated on that damn biker bar, so much so that when it sold, he begged my dad to buy it. Dad wanted him to take over the construction business, but Mick was adamant that if he bought the bar, he'd straighten up and fly right. Instead, he just drank more. Then, when things came to blows with the family about it, he ran away."

Running away? Was it possible I inherited this trait from him?

Max, as if reading my mind, said, "I'll leave you to it, but I just wanted to tell you that I've never looked at you and seen any Finley in you, physically or otherwise."

I swallowed. "You haven't?"

"No. Not at all. I hope you find what you're looking for."

I smiled. "Thanks, Max."

He turned and walked out of the garage, and I was left with a little inkling of hope. I dug back into my mother's things, but after going through all three of the boxes, I didn't find anything to prove or disprove Mickey was my father, and there was no sign of Sonny's birth certificate either.

By the time I went back inside, the day was half over and I was no closer to resolving things. I got back into bed and pulled the covers over my head. I must have fallen asleep because I could see Grammy standing behind the kitchen island again. I was asking her about me and Sonny being twins. She told me to check the reference shelf.

Chapter Twenty-Eight

I jolted awake and sat up. *Check the reference shelf.*
I had completely forgotten to do that earlier when the smoke detector went off. Still groggy and reeling from getting a visit from Grammy, I got up and splashed some water on my face. While I patted it dry with the towel, I smelled something odd in the air. I sniffed again. What was that? It seemed to be wafting up from the kitchen. Was the burned bacon smell still hanging around? Or was somebody cooking?

I headed down the stairs and saw GG standing in front of the stove. "What time is it?"

"Nearly five. You okay?" he asked.

"I just took a nap. What are you doing?"

"I made dinner."

"You did?"

"Yeah."

"What is it?"

"House special."

"House special?"

"Spaghetti," he said, turning to face me. "Will you set the table? It's almost done."

"Spaghetti?" I asked, inhaling again. I guess it did smell a little like spaghetti.

"It's the only thing I can cook."

The jury was still out on that. "You must be starving. You should have come and got me."

"No. You needed your rest. Now, get the table set, and let me concentrate on the finishing touches."

I couldn't imagine what the finishing touches were going to be, but I went to the buffet and grabbed the dishes. As I set the table, I eyeballed the reference shelf again. I wanted to go over and start searching for the birth certificate, but I didn't have time. GG was already yelling for me to come and carry stuff. He was getting around pretty well now with just a cast and his cane, but he wouldn't be able to carry something and walk with the cane.

"Can you bring this pot of noodles to the table?"

"Sure. You go sit down. I can do this."

He nodded and I glanced at the food. It looked like spaghetti noodles and red sauce. And it smelled like it, too. I wasn't sure why I was so suspicious, except that I'd never seen GG cook a thing and he was nearly eighty years old. But I carried it to the table and we dished it up.

"I hope it's edible," he said.

I took a tentative bite. "It's good," I said, relieved. "I was worried because…what is that smell?"

"The secret ingredient."

"Which is?"

"Wouldn't be a secret if I told you, would it?"

I set my fork down in protest.

"Fine. It's just apple cider."

"Apple cider?"

"In the sauce. My mother added it to everything. We were apple farmers."

"Oh." I took another taste. "Interesting. I can taste it now. It's not bad."

"Right?"

"When's the last time you cooked?"

"When I was a boy I did a lot of cooking, actually. But I liked spaghetti best. Easy. Fast. Filling."

"I'm surprised you remember how after all these years."

"Oh, I had to relearn when Ida got sick. She was still trying to cook until the day I took her to the hospital, but I kept shooing her out of the kitchen. At first, I made a lot of soup from cans, but then I tried the spaghetti again after I couldn't tolerate another bite of soup. I'm old, but not that old."

I laughed and cried at the same time. "I miss Grammy," I blurted out. "I had a dream about her when I was napping just now."

He nodded. "She's visited me a few times, too. It's just like her to check up on us. Will she ever rest?"

We laughed again and GG blew his nose into a hanky that I happened to notice had Grammy's initials on it. I wondered if he'd taken the one from her night table as a means to keep her close, which had been my exact thought when I saw it sitting there. That made my heart melt and then I had to blow my nose into my own napkin.

When we were done, GG retired to his chair to read the paper and I went outside for some air. As I wandered the property to clear my head, I found myself in the orchard in front of the tree where Grammy and Sonny were laid to rest. It was a scraggly old tree that stood out from the rest because it had a funny little bend in the trunk that made it sort of lean to one side more. It was the tree that Sonny and I had swatted at with sticks because the apples hung in a tempting way. Now I was able to stand under it and plunk them from the bud without lifting my arms. They weren't ready to do so yet.

They were hardly bigger than cherries now.

As I weaved through the handful of trees, I had a short conversation with Grammy in my head. I asked her for help. I wished she were still here to give it to me. I didn't know what to do. Was my sister not my sister? What was Mom covering up? Was the birth certificate the missing link here? I stopped and leaned up against one of the trees while I let the quiet settle around me. I thought maybe my dream, Grammy's wisdom, would become more clear if I just emptied all of the clutter from my brain so I could absorb the message she was sending, but I waited until the mosquitos began to infiltrate and I was forced back into the house without acquiring any more knowledge than what I had before I arrived at the orchard.

When GG went to bed, I turned the lamp on near the bookcase and I began to pull out the books and photo albums, sifting through them, shaking the pages out upside down, hoping something would fall out. It felt like a longshot, but then suddenly something did fall out. It was a white piece of paper, folded in half. It fluttered from the pages of one of the albums. I'd gone through the albums with a fine-toothed comb recently and hadn't seen the certificate, so it had to have been wedged in between one of the pages and the clear sticky backing.

I knew from the weight and color of the cardstock that it was exactly what I was looking for: Sonny's birth certificate.

I unfolded it feeling hopeful that the answers I'd been seeking would all be made clear, but as I read the document, my hope faded. It listed Sonny's name, date, time, and place of birth. Just like mine, it listed Jennifer Ann Andersen as my mother and where the father's name was supposed to go, it was blank. But it didn't take long for me to confirm that we were born on the same date, just a few minutes apart, but we were indeed twins.

I sunk down, putting my back to the shelf. I was so conflicted. I was relieved to find out that Sonny was my twin. I had no idea why it mattered so much to me, but it did. It didn't help prove or disprove anything beyond that, but at least my entire life wasn't a lie.

I didn't understand why Sonny's birth certificate was in such an odd place. I considered putting it back into the safe with the rest of the family documents, but I supposed it didn't really need to be locked up for safe keeping anymore.

For whatever reason, I carried it along with me to my bedroom and set it next to me on the dresser. When I lay down, I closed my eyes, wishing for sleep to come to me so I didn't have to see my mother's paintings in my head anymore. I didn't want to think about any of this for the next six to eight hours. I wanted the week to speed up so I could talk to my mother and get some answers.

I hoped maybe Grammy would visit my dreams again, but instead, I had a nightmare. I shot up, sweat-soaked, with my heart thumping so hard it almost shook the bed. My head was spinning, like I'd had too much to drink, but I hadn't been drinking. I got up and opened the window to let some air in. It was still dark out. I went down the hall and into the bathroom thinking I might be sick, because for the first time in my entire life, I remembered the nightmare upon waking. It was so clear. I splashed water on my face, trying to wake up more, so the image would leave me, but it was still there. I wasn't sure why I hadn't seen it until now. Those blood-soaked scenes, the point-of-view of the one person who'd been there to see the whole thing. She was painting with blood. It soaked her brush, the walls, as well as the canvases. And when she turned I saw her face too.

It was my mother.

I crept quietly down the stairs knowing I wasn't going to be doing anymore sleeping, even if it was too early for the rooster to have made a noise yet. I made a pot of coffee. When it was done, I took a cup onto the porch and watched the early morning light spread out across the fields. I had missed this aspect of Alton when I was in New York. The smell of dew on the grass, the sounds of the animals starting to stir in and around the barn, I tried to take it all in and replace the feeling of dread still lingering from the nightmare. Because that was all it was. A bad dream. It wasn't real. It couldn't be real.

All I wanted to do was get away. I abandoned my coffee, which was only contributing to my jitters, and I went into the garage and saw my old ten-speed bike on a peg. I pulled it down. The tires were flat, but the bike was otherwise in pretty good shape. I found the old bike pump and gave the tires some air. I hadn't ridden a bike since I'd last been on this one, but if the old saying was correct, it would be just like riding a bike.

I went back to the house, scribbled a quick note for GG in case he wondered where I was when he got up and then I got on the bike and pedaled away from the farm as fast as I could. Once I got out onto Upper Alton Road, I was able to coast downhill most of the way without slowing down until I reached the river. I set the bike down in the sand beside me and I sat down trying to slow my breathing.

The water was still for a change. Everything was

calm and quiet. It was even too early for fishing, so the boats were all docked. I absorbed the tranquility, knowing it wouldn't last. I pulled my phone out and I opened Brad's contact information. It was still so early, I hated to wake him. On the other hand, he'd come to the farm to bring the casserole that morning really early. My finger hovered over the call button until I finally pushed it.

"Are you okay?" were the first words out of his mouth. I could hear him breathing heavily.

"Did I wake you? I…"

"No. It's fine. What's wrong?"

"I had a nightmare. My mom was the one. She did it."

"What?"

I was crying now and my breathing was so fast, I worried I might hyperventilate. "In the dream, she killed Robbie and Sonny. She had literal blood on her hands, and everywhere else. It was…just like in the red shed."

"Okay. Try to take it easy. Luna. Listen to me. It was just a bad dream. That's all."

"But…what if it's true? I hadn't even considered it but…it makes sense. She was there when her brother died and she was there when Sonny…"

"Why would she kill Sonny? Her own child? What reason would she have for doing that?"

"I don't know. It happens. I've seen stories on the news about mothers going crazy and drowning their babies."

"Okay, but then why did she not kill you too? It doesn't make sense. And her brother? She was just a kid, right? Why would she want her brother to die? Even if she did, she couldn't force him on that combine. That's impossible. Listen…I know your mom is a little…unstable, but I highly doubt she murdered anyone."

My breathing slowed a little.

I sniffled. "You're probably right. I'm just so confused. All I know is that I saw her in the dream and it suddenly all made sense."

"I know. I think you probably just manifested it because of the paintings, but she painted those after the fact because she was likely incredibly traumatized by what she saw. It was her way of making sense of things."

I nodded. "I just still have so many questions. Like why was Mickey there that night? If he's our father, then that makes sense, but if that's true, then where does Jeffrey Donovan fit in? And why were they arguing? I just want to know the truth, you know?"

"Yeah. I understand. Where are you?"

"At the river."

"Do you want me to come and sit with you?"

"You don't have to do that. I feel much better. You've helped enough just talking me through it. I'm sorry for waking you up."

"That's what I'm here for. Hey…why don't you come by the bar later. I'll be there all night. It will be a good distraction."

"I will."

"You promise?"

"Yes. I promise."

"Okay. I'll see you then."

"And…Brad? Thank you."

"It's what friends-potential cousins-potential… it's what people do for people they love."

"You…love me?"

"I've loved you since the first time we ran off together and hid in the hay loft when we were eight when we were supposed to be feeding the chickens. When we came down you had straw in your hair. I knew it was a dead giveaway. I wanted to pick it out, but I was too shy about touching you, so I left it."

"I remember that. Instead, when your dad asked where we'd been, you took the blame for it."

He laughed.

"I don't know what I'd do without you," I said.

"Lucky for you, you're stuck with me."

"Are you sure? Because…look at what a mess I am. If you want to back out now, I wouldn't blame you. You didn't know when you signed up for this."

He laughed. "Yeah. I actually did. And I'm sure."

Chapter Twenty-Nine

Pedaling the bike back up the hills of Alton was much harder now than going down it and it was even worse now than when I was a kid. The sun had warmed and I had to get off the bike and push it just as I came upon the little white church. Now would be a perfect time to go inside and talk to God. Maybe if I repented my sins all of this would stop.

It was still early. I had no idea if the place would even be open, but Daniel had said that I could pop in anytime I needed to talk. I pushed my bicycle and leaned it alongside the stucco building and found the front door of the church. I pushed on it a little and it opened right up. Stepping in, it was dark and quiet. I wasn't sure if I should even be here, but I went to the back row of pews and I sat down.

Now what? I could pray but that didn't feel quite right. Instead, I just sat, thinking, taking in the light that shone down from the stained glass window. I didn't even think about whether or not my mom was responsible for the deaths of her brother and my sister. Instead, I thought about Brad and how he made me feel. It was probably terribly wrong to be thinking about that while sitting in the house of the Lord, but that was what came to my mind when I sat down to think. I thought about how I felt so much better after calling him, about how I didn't feel like I was alone in this mess as long as I had him. I thought about how he'd told me he loved me.

"Miss Andersen? Is that you?"

I turned to see Daniel coming in. I stood up, realizing I was covered in sweat from the bike ride. "Hi. Yeah. It's Luna."

"Right," he said, smacking his forehead with his palm. "Luna. How are you?"

"I'm doing okay."

"Are you sure? Because it's not even eight in the morning and you're here talking to God."

"Yeah. I just...well, I had a bad dream and I needed some guidance."

He smiled. "Ah. Well, God is the best guidance."

I nodded.

"Did you want to talk about it at all? I have a little time."

"Oh, you know what? I think I'm good now."

"Are you sure?" he asked.

"Yeah. God took care of it," I said with a light laugh.

He snapped his fingers. "He beat me to it, I guess."

"I should actually be heading out."

"It was nice to see you," Daniel said.

"You too."

Back outside, I grabbed my bike, hopped on, and started to pedal away. As I huffed up the last leg of the hill, I tried to shake off the fact that I'd straight up lied to a religious man. God took care of it. What was I thinking? God hadn't taken care of it. Brad had.

By the time I reached the farm, my legs felt like noodles and my clothes were soaked in sweat. It was still so early that GG was just starting to stir when I came in. I got in the shower and tried to wash the terror and humiliation off of me. Not only about the incident at the church, but also about showing Brad how truly broken I was. But at the same time, I was now more sure than ever that I had feelings for him, and if we were going to pursue things, he needed to see what he was getting. I wasn't a prize. I was more like a used car. I needed heavy repairs in order to run properly. I was missing parts and nobody had replacements. It reminded me of when I wanted to tell Ernie about Mom's issues. It was only fair. And the fact that Brad was still willing to take a chance on me made my heart flutter.

Though I felt much better, the nightmare hadn't totally dissipated from my mind. Brad was probably right about it being a manifestation, but I still wanted more proof. It was the only way to settle my anxiety. How was I going to get proof though?

While I made GG some pancakes, he came down.

"Mornin', Lu."

I poured him coffee and set his plate down.

"Aren't you eating?"

"I'm not very hungry."

He grunted.

I sat down across from him at the oak table. "Can I ask you something?"

Another grunt.

"I've been thinking about those paintings, with Mom and Robbie. I know it's probably hard to talk about but what happened…to him? I know he was on the combine, but why? What was he doing? Was he alone when it happened? How old was he?"

GG took a sip of his coffee. "Your uncle Robert was a precocious kid. He wanted to grow up faster than time was letting him. He was nine. I let him help out as much as he was capable at the time, but he wanted to do more.

Farming was in his blood, but he was a skinny, hyper child. Jenny would follow him around and tell him to be careful, because he was always getting hurt. He broke an arm at five when he fell out of an apple tree. He cracked his head open at seven when he tried to shimmy down the well."

"Was my mom with him when these things happened?"

"No. If she would have been, they probably would not have happened. Back then…before the accident, your mom was more…like you, really. She was cautious and smart. She was always telling Robert to mind this, don't do that." GG laughed. "Sometimes he would get so mad at her. And apparently, according to Jenny, that day was one of those days. They'd argued. He wanted to do something exciting. She wanted to sit quietly with her drawing. Who does that remind you of? I was out in the far east fields that day planting and come supper time, Robbie was nowhere to be seen, so Gram whistled for him. I was just starting back when I heard your mom shrieking like a banshee. I went into the pole barn and that's when I saw. She was cradling her brother in her arms. She was covered in blood. It was…a bad scene."

"That's…awful," I said.

"She blamed herself, your mother, but if anybody should have been blamed, it was me," he said. "I can't count the times I'd told him that he was not allowed on the equipment unless I was with him, but he was just so eager. Seemed like the more I said no, the more he wanted to do it. And after that, well, your mother changed. Can't blame her, really. She was angry. She'd lost her best friend."

I nodded, realizing that I could relate to that.

I went upstairs and took out the notepad of my mother's that I'd found earlier and I flipped through the pages again. Had Ernie been right? Had I been wrong to blame my mother all this time? I stopped at another poem that I'd missed the first time I'd looked through the pages.

Detasseling

Two stalks of corn blossom in the light of the golden prairie,

Side by side,
They are one, they are whole.
Not boy, nor girl,
Each with tassels
Until one is plucked.
Removed, it divides them.
One male.
One female.
They become pollinated, hybridized.
Such is the process of life.
We are born.
We are one.
We are pulled apart.
Then we are gone.

****

That night, I made us some dinner, got myself together to go to the bar for a bit, and said goodbye to GG while he was still on the porch with his pipe and newspaper.

"You look nice," he said. "Going somewhere special?"

"Just to Finley's. I'll be back early, but call me if you need anything."

"I won't."

"But if you do…"

"I won't. Have fun, kiddo."

"Goodnight, Grandpa."

"Night, Lu."

****

I walked into the bar and thought about how funny it was that just a few months ago I came in full of trepidation about seeing Brad, and today I looked forward to spending some time chatting with him. The place felt less dark and confining than that first night. I was even starting to recognize some of the people sitting at the bar from the previous times I'd been in. Kelsey was waiting on customers at a booth and she looked over and waved as I made my way toward Brad.

"Hey," he said with a concerned smile. "How are you doing?"

"I'm better."

"You look good."

I smiled. "I feel surprisingly good, which is actually maybe a bad sign because the last time I thought things were good, they all went straight to hell in a handbasket."

Brad opened a Hart's for me and poured it into a pint glass. I didn't stop him because I kinda liked the idea of having a usual.

"So, guess what…I have some news," he said.

I took a sip of my drink. "Yeah? What?"

"Uncle Kenny and my dad made some calls around to various family members, and they were able to locate Mick. He retired from trucking and has settled down in…"

I didn't know if it was simply the topic of Mickey that triggered it, or what it was, but the room immediately began closing in around me.

"Luna? Are you okay?"

"I…" I put my head down on the bar and closed my eyes, trying to breath, trying to keep myself from fading away further. My chest felt like a pile of bricks was sitting on top of it. Brad came around to the other side of the bar and rubbed my back. Kelsey must have come over too because I heard him faintly talking to her. "Will you get a cold compress? Some water? Bring it into the office for me, please."

"Can you walk?" he asked me.

Somehow I must have done it because when I opened my eyes back up, I was lying on a couch in a small room. A cool cloth was draped on my forehead.

"Hey…there you are," Brad said from a chair next to me.

"I'm so sorry."

"Don't be. Have a sip of water." He held the glass to my mouth and I took a sip.

Suddenly, I understood. "I think I know what keeps triggering me."

"What?" he asked.

"I think it's the Hart's."

"Huh?"

"When I was here one night Kelsey told me that your family used to refer to Hart's as Uncle Mickeys. I wonder if the smell of it is connecting my brain to that night when he was there in the apartment. Or other times he was around us when we were little. It adds up because the first night I was here and I ordered one, it happened, and when we were sixteen on the hill when you kissed me we were drinking Hart's."

"Huh. But what about that time when we were playing hide and seek? That didn't involve any beer. We were too young."

"No. I figured that out too. It was the blanket. That afghan was draped over my head when I saw Sonny get shot. It's a trigger too. That's also probably why I never had any panic attacks in New York. I didn't have a single Hart's and the blankie was still back at the farm. So it wasn't Alton causing the attacks after all. It was the trauma from seeing Sonny die. I'm no therapist, but I'm guessing those things spark my brain to almost turn off instead of letting me experience the whole terrible thing again."

"Wow. That's crazy, but it does make sense."

And then I remembered what he was telling me just before the attack hit and I sat up. "Wait. You located Mickey?"

He nodded. "He's living in Iowa in a small town just outside of Waterloo. I mapped it. It's not that far from here, only about a three and a half hour drive."

"Really?"

"I have the day off tomorrow. We could go and talk to him, I mean, if that's what you want to do."

"It is! I hate asking you to come with me, but...I would really like it if you did."

"Are you kidding? I love a good road trip," he said with a goofy smile.

"Yeah? I hear Iowa is beautiful this time of year."

He laughed. "You sure you're going to be okay doing this?"

"Yeah. I need to get this figured out."

"Right. Okay. I better get back out there. If you want to stay here and rest some more..."

"No. I'm good now. I think I'll just stick with the water though."

213

"Great idea. No more Hart's for you."

We went back out to the bar. I sat and finished my water and waited for the full effects of the panic attack to subside before Brad walked me out to GG's truck.

"So, I'll pick you up tomorrow morning around eight," he said. "I'll send a text to my dad and ask him to keep an eye on Gus while we're gone."

"You've thought of everything," I said.

"Well, not everything."

"Oh?"

"You're in charge of road snacks."

"Got it," I said with a laugh. "I'm paying for the gas, too."

"We'll see."

I opened the door of the truck and we lingered in the shadow of the flickering bulb of the dingy street lamp. "I really hope he's not my dad, by the way. And that's saying something because I've always thought finding my dad was the most important thing there was."

"We'll know by tomorrow afternoon," he said.

"I can't wait. I'll see you tomorrow."

Chapter Thirty

Brad pulled into the driveway at 7:59. I had already made GG some breakfast and fixed him a sandwich for later. I briefed him over oatmeal what I was doing. He wasn't very fond of the whole plan, but he understood why I was doing it. I kissed him on the cheek and told him that I'd be home late. He told me to be careful and reminded me for the third time that he had a doctor's appointment the following morning. I told him I'd be back in time to take him to his appointment.

I ran out and hopped into Brad's car feeling like I was sixteen again happy to be driving away from the farm.

"Does it feel weird to be leaving Alton?" I teased as we got onto the ramp to the freeway.

"I have left the town before, you know?"

"What's the farthest you've been from here?"

"I backpacked in Europe the summer after you moved to New York and graduated."

"Really? You did?"

"Yep. I was gone for four months, went to France, Switzerland, England, Scotland, and Ireland."

"Wow. That's cool."

"It was interesting."

"And after that, you still decided that Alton was the best place for you, huh?"

"Honestly? Yeah. I did. I like Alton."

"Why exactly?"

"I'm content here. I like the comfort and peace and quiet. I like being near my family, having their support."

"I didn't have any of those things in Alton."

"I suppose that's true. What do you like about New York?"

"I mean…after being so sheltered on the farm, I liked the hustle and bustle of the city, but mostly I just wanted to be somewhere else. It wasn't really about New York because I did miss the green space and the river. I just don't like feeling so…trapped."

"You make it sound like you aren't free to come and go, but look at us…we're leaving." He laughed. "You know, I think you're associating small towns with small aspirations, but it doesn't have to be like that. For instance, I bet you didn't know that I've been taking classes online and I'm just six months shy of getting my MBA."

"Really? I didn't know that."

"You sound surprised," he said.

"Maybe, a little, yes."

We pulled into a gas station and I went inside to load up on the promised road snacks. I also paid for the gas while Brad was still pumping. Once we got onto the freeway, we busted open the chips and drove for a while without talking.

A few hours into the drive, I started to get nervous about what exactly we would find when we arrived at Mickey's. "How much do you know about your uncle?" I asked Brad.

"Well, even though he left Alton before I was born, the family did talk about him a lot, or at least the lore of him. He was the mysterious guy that everyone wanted to

216

discuss. And, you'll probably think it's stupid, but I would flip through pictures when I was at Grandpa Bob and Grandma Betty's house when I was little and I remember thinking Mickey was so cool looking. And that's why I started to drink the Hart's when I was young. Because at holidays everyone would pass the cans around and toast to Uncle Mickey, because he was apparently always drinking a Hart's beer. It was also the reason why I asked if I could run the bar, much to my father's dismay. But after a little while, I realized it wasn't all that it was cracked up to be. You probably didn't know this about me either, but I'm two years sober."

"Really? Isn't it hard to work at a bar then? And be around it all the time?"

"It doesn't bother me. If anything, it reminds me of why I've chosen not to."

"Why have you?" I asked.

"I realized I was basically just using alcohol to avoid the hard stuff I was pushing down, like the death of my mom and sister. So, I went to therapy and dealt with it all properly, and now, the whole allure of alcohol is gone for me. I just don't see the need for it anymore. I want other things for myself."

"Wow. The things you can learn about a person while driving for miles with only corn fields is really astonishing."

"What about you? What are your goals?" he asked.

"I mean…you make me feel bad about myself now because yeah, I haven't really dealt with my own issues either. And I could stand to cut back on drinking some too."

"Okay, but I didn't mean it like that. I was just

asking about your long-term goals. You know, big picture stuff."

"Ah. Hmm. Well, I'd like to not only illustrate other people's children's books, but I want to one day write my own story to go along with the drawings too."

"Oh, yeah?"

"Yeah."

"That's cool."

"Thanks."

I couldn't help but continue falling deeper and deeper for the person in the driver's seat, even though I knew it might lead to utter heartbreak within the matter of another hour or so. Brad must have been having the same thoughts because he turned the radio on, dug back into the snacks and we drove the last stretch without saying much of anything.

When we came into Waterloo, I immediately started to hum the tune with the same name while navigating us through the downtown until we got to a small neighborhood on the outskirts.

My anxiety started to peak as we wound our way, searching for the correct house number. We stopped in front of a small toothpaste green rambler with a big, unwelcoming fence running the length of the property on the sides and around the back.

"You feeling okay?" Brad asked me as we parked on the street in front of the house.

"Not really, but we're here, so…"

We got out and not two steps from the car, a cacophony of angry barking broke out from behind the privacy fence.

"This doesn't bode well," I said as we stopped at the door. Apprehensively, I knocked. After a second, someone yelled from the other side, through the barking, "I'm not buying anything. Go away!"

"Uncle Mickey?" Brad hollered back. "It's Brad Finley, Max's son."

There was a delay before the door cracked open. "Brad?" he said. "What the hell are you doing here?"

"We were traveling through Waterloo and we thought we'd say hello," he lied.

The door opened a crack further. A man who looked much older than someone in his early sixties stood before us. Overweight and weathered looking, he was less intimidating than I had imagined him to be. His hair was no longer long, but it was still more or less dark and he still had some facial hair too. The piercing eyes were still alert and familiar too. And I took a few deep breaths trying to stay calm and not lose it completely.

He scrutinized us for a minute. "You're Max's kid, huh?"

"Yeah. And this is Luna. Could we come in?"

"Yeah. Okay." He opened the door. The dogs continued to let their presence be known until he yelled, "Shut up!" And then they went quiet.

We stepped into the living room. It was dated and compact, but cleaner than I had anticipated. There was a small loveseat and a recliner facing a large flat-screen. A TV tray like the ones Grammy had from the 1970s was propped next to it. On it an ashtray sat filled with ash and cigarette butts, and a half drunk bottle of soda was next to that. Mickey sat down in the recliner. Brad and I stayed standing.

"What brings you to Waterloo?" he asked.

"Well, to be honest, we had a couple of questions for you."

"What kind of questions?"

"I…am Jenny Andersen's daughter," I finally said.

He glanced up at me for a second. "So?"

I tensed up. "So…I was wondering…if you think…I might…could I be your daughter?"

His whole face contorted and his head started to move from side to side. "I did have a daughter with Jenny, but she died. Her name was Sonny."

Brad and I exchanged confused looks, but I pushed on. "Okay…but, I'm her sister."

"I only had the one kid with Jenny."

"Luna is Sonny's twin sister," Brad said, carefully.

Mickey looked up at me again, studying me. "No. That's impossible. I never knew nothing about no twin sister. I only knew Sonny." His voice got louder, "Are you taking me for a ride, because…"

I opened my purse and pulled out both birth certificates and held them out toward him. He snatched them from my hand and looked them over. "I don't know what to tell ya," he said before handing me back the papers. "I was drinking pretty heavily back then but I think I would have remembered having two daughters, twins at that."

"Can I ask you, what you were doing there that night?"

He pulled a pack of cigarettes out of the front pocket of his shirt and he lit it. After a few puffs, he said, "I came to see my kid. Jenny didn't want to let me in, but she was my kid too, and I had a right to see her."

"And then there was a fight?"

"Something like that. I don't remember the exact details. Like I said, I'd been drinking."

"And you'd had visits with her before that night?"

"Sure. Jenny and I were trying to make a go of it. We were always hot and cold." He blew out more smoke and a hazy cloud sat heavy in the air between us.

The room started to spin and I took another deep breath, but that didn't help much because all I took in was second-hand smoke. Brad took my hand. "You okay? You look a little pale. Here, sit down for a second." He led me to the love seat.

"She all right?" Mickey asked, with a softer tone now.

"She has some trauma around this whole thing," he said. "She was there that night…that her sister died. She saw it all happen," I heard Brad explain.

"I can help with that," Mickey said. "Here." He pulled something else from his other top shirt pocket. I couldn't really see what it was. A tube of something. "Just dab a little under her nose."

I took another breath and the smell of peppermint hit me, jolting me back to reality. My chest even loosened up. I must have looked shocked by the revelation.

"It works, right?" Mickey said, smiling at me.

"What is it?"

"Just peppermint extract. An old army vet told me about it."

"It…I feel so much better," I said. "Thank you."

He nodded. "You can keep that one. I've got more."

"So you have panic attacks too?" I asked him.

He nodded. "I'd say you inherited from me, but I get them for the same reason as you. I get flashbacks, little snippets of that night."

"You didn't have them until then?"

"Nope. It'll sober you right up to see your child get shot in front of your eyes."

Brad was still holding my hand, stroking it.

"Oh, I see what's going on," Mickey said. "You two are…I can see it on your faces. You want to know if I'm her dad because you're in love, but you're my nephew, so if she's mine, then you two might be cousins. Am I right?"

Brad released my hand. "Something like that," he said.

He looked back to me. "Well, I wish I could help you out, but I don't know if you're my kid or not."

"I understand," I said. "My mom seemed to be playing some games."

Mickey shrugged. "Don't be too hard on her. She had a rough go of things herself. That was why she and I connected back in school. We both felt like misfits. And it being a small town didn't make things any easier. Everybody knowing yer business. Neither of us fit in, in Alton or in our own families."

I wanted to argue with him. My grandparents hadn't done anything to make my mother not feel welcome in their home. I was sure of that.

But before I could, he asked Brad, "How's Max doing, by the way?"

"He's good."

"Still a farmer?"

"Yep."

"Who's running the bar now?"

"Me and Kelsey, Kenny's daughter."

"Is that right? Is it doing well?"

"Not too bad."

"Good for you." He took another drag of his cigarette before he put it out in the ashtray. "I don't know what else to tell you. I've said everything I know about

Sonny. I'm guessing you'll have to talk to Jenny to find out what was going on."

I nodded. "Thanks for talking with us."

"Let me give you my number. I would like to know what's going on too when you find out. If you're mine, then I want to get to know you better."

I took out my phone and put his contact info into it. "I really appreciate it." I stood up slowly. "And for this," I held up the peppermint oil. "Can I give you a hug?"

"Why not?" He got up and we hugged. He and Brad hugged too. "Okay, you kids take care. I hope everything works out for you, even if it means that I lose another daughter," he said with a chuckle.

"We will," Brad said, opening the door. "You too, Uncle Mickey. And, if you're ever passing through Alton, don't be a stranger."

"Nobody is ever just passing through Alton," Mickey said. "But, yeah, okay. And tell Max I said hello, would ya?"

"Sure thing."

When we got back into the car, Brad looked at me. "Well, that was interesting."

"To say the least. But we still have no definitive answers. I'm so sorry that you brought me all this way for nothing," I said.

He started the car up. "I was really hoping you'd finally have some closure. But you know what? I'm still glad we came."

"You are?"

"Sure. Besides, it wasn't for nothing. You did learn one thing."

"What?"

"That the peppermint oil helps with the attacks."

"Yes. That is pretty useful."
"You ready to go?"
"Alton or bust," I said.
Brad smiled and we were off.

Chapter Thirty-One

We stopped at a truck stop for some food on the way home.

I ordered pancakes and realized that was my go-to food for iffy restaurants when I was too hungry to risk anything. When Brad also ordered pancakes, I gave him a look.

"What?" he asked.

"I don't know. For some reason, I didn't peg you for a pancake guy."

"What kinda guy did you peg me for, Luna Andersen?"

"Hmm...I was thinking more like a ham and cheese omelet."

"That's so...specific and a little weird."

"I thought you knew that about me by now, Bradley Finley."

"I forgot, but it's coming back. It's definitely part of your intrigue."

"Oh, I have intrigue?"

He nodded. "Most definitely, which is another reason why I'm pretty sure you aren't a Finley. We have no intrigue. People can guess exactly what we usually order at a truck stop just by looking at us."

I laughed. The food came and while we ate it, I said, "Okay, so what's your take on this whole situation with Mickey? Because I'm just...not sure what to think about him."

"Well, the fact that he'd never seen or heard of you makes me think you aren't his kid, because why would your mom bother to tell him about Sonny and not you? And then the whole Night and Day thing…it seems like she knew."

"I don't see how that's possible."

"I don't know either, and no offense, but I think she was dating more than one guy."

"Jeffrey Donovan being one of them," I realized.

"Yeah. It sounds like Mickey wanted to see Sonny and your mom wasn't having it."

"Maybe because Mickey hadn't been told about the other guy and he showed up unannounced?"

"Right." Brad nodded. "So, if she hadn't told Mickey about him, then Jeff most likely didn't know about Mickey either."

"So, she told him someone was trying to break in," we both said in unison.

Brad's eyes got wide. "Okay. That was a little weird."

"So, Jeffrey thought Mickey was a robber…"

"And from a biker gang," Brad added.

"Yeah. Unbelievable. And if that's all true, then it sort of does make my mom responsible."

"Let's not jump to too many conclusions. We could be completely wrong here," Brad said.

"God. I honestly hope we are."

****

I offered to drive when we got back in the car, but Brad refused to let me. I still felt unsettled considering things weren't totally clear yet. However, it seemed like I was inching closer and closer. It was like all of the puzzle pieces were on the table, now I just needed to wedge them into the correct spots to see the full picture.

"What day are your mom and Ernie coming home?" Brad asked.

"Late Saturday, I think. I was invited over to their place for brunch and a gift opening party on Sunday morning, so I guess after everyone leaves the party, I'll have a chance to talk to my mom and find out what the hell is going on."

"How are you going to get her to tell you the truth?" he asked.

"I don't know. I've been trying my whole life and I've yet to succeed. I'm clearly dealing with a pro too. She's been manipulating more people than just me for years."

"Yeah. You need a strategy."

"I was hoping you had one for me," I said.

"What if you don't tell her we went to see Mickey, but instead tell her about us? You could say that you aren't going to pursue anything though because you figured out that Mickey was there and you know there's a chance he could be your father."

"Hmm. I'm not sure that will work because she seems fine with us not dating."

"Oh, good point."

"I need something that forces her to talk, something that shows her I've caught her in something."

"Okay. So, what if you try to bluff her. Tell her you did find Mickey and that you went to see him. Act like you know the truth already."

"Unless she knows that Mickey doesn't know the truth."

"Except, Mickey did say that he believed Sonny was

his daughter."

"True. That might work," I said. "It's better than my only idea."

"What's that?"

"Nothing."

Brad laughed. "No wonder you still don't know who your dad is."

"I know. I'd laugh, but at this point, I'd rather cry."

"Hey, have you ever tried that one with your mom? Bursting into tears?"

"Yep. Loads of times. Didn't work obviously."

****

When we reached the farm, it was early evening and we were both wiped out from the long drive and the rollercoaster events of the day. I thanked Brad over and over again. Since I had to get up early to take GG to his appointment, we said goodnight. I watched him back down the driveway before I went inside.

I found GG safe and sound, hunched over his workbench tinkering with something or other.

"I'm back," I told him. "Did you eat dinner?"

Without looking up, he said, "Yep. Made my specialty."

"More spaghetti?"

"A man's gotta eat."

"No offense, kiddo, but I'm getting kinda sick of sandwiches. Did you find your dad?"

"I don't know. Mickey seemed to think Sonny was his daughter, but he didn't even know I existed. That's strange, right?"

GG grunted. "I wouldn't buy anything he says."

I nodded. "Which is why I still don't know who my dad is."

"And how was he? Was he decent?"

"He wasn't as bad as I thought he might be. Why exactly didn't you and Grammy like him?"

"He was rude, directionless, and drank too much. And he had no respect for us or your mother."

"I think he may be sober now."

GG cleared his throat. "That's good."

"Yeah. Well, you better come inside and get some sleep. We need to get up early tomorrow."

"I'll be in shortly."

"Okay."

I went inside and put the kettle on for tea. I thought maybe it would help me sleep better. As I waited for the water to come to a boil, I stood at the counter looking at the reference shelf, thinking about Grammy and the time I asked her what fraternal meant. From this perspective, the dream I had a few nights prior also floated into the mix. My answer had been in the dictionary that time in my youth and I realized it was also the dictionary I was pulling out in my dream. Just for the hell of it, I went over to the shelf and pulled the dictionary out, just like I had done when I was a little girl trying to understand how Sonny and I were connected as twins, just as Grammy had advised me to do.

I set the book on the dining room table and flipped the pages until I came to the F section and found the word *fraternal*. I read the definition. It hadn't changed in the last ten years, but I noticed that below it, is said, also see *twin*. I went to the *T*s and read the definition for twins. Below that definition, it said, also see: *identical* and *superfecundation*.

Superfecundation? What was that? I quickly found it and read the definition: *When two or more ova are fertilized by separate acts of sexual intercourse.*

I read it over and over again trying to process it. Could this have anything to do with me and Sonny? Was this actually what Grammy had been directing me toward in the dream? I pulled my phone out and snapped a picture of the word and definition so I would remember it. Just as I closed the book, the kettle began to whistle, causing me to jump.

I took my tea out to the porch and sipped it as the sun crept lower in the sky. I thought about everything that had happened and then tried to put it out of my mind. It was still going to be a long couple of days before my mom returned and I needed to get some rest before then. As I finished my tea, I listened for GG to come inside. When I heard the back door open and close, I relaxed a little and waited for the tea to kick in and start making me sleepy. Sitting on the porch swing, day turned to night and I noticed the moon. It was cut right down the middle. A half-moon. I could relate. Luna. I often felt like a girl who wasn't whole.

Chapter Thirty-Two

When the rooster crowed, it was so ungodly early, but I came to, rolled over, and realized I'd sleep straight through the night without a single nightmare. I got up and stretched out my back. It was sore from the long car ride coupled with the old, thin mattress on the bed, but besides that, I felt rested. As I arched my back and lifted my arms, I peered out the window trying to get a sense of the day ahead. The clouds appeared heavy. I hoped there wasn't a storm brewing.

GG was already in the kitchen starting the coffee when I came down the stairs.

"Morning," I said. "You must be up early because you're excited to go to the doctor," I joked.

"I'm excited to get this blasted anchor removed from my foot."

"It's not guaranteed. Fia said they would do some X-rays first to see if everything is looking healed up."

"She's a friend of yours, right? Can't you pull some strings?"

"No! You don't want to have permanent damage and not be able to walk well, do you?"

He grunted. "If it means getting this torture device off sooner? Maybe."

"You don't mean that."

"Fine," he grumbled.

After a quick breakfast, we headed over to the clinic.

This time we were a bit early, so GG had nothing to complain about to the nurses. He seemed to be on his best behavior, like that would somehow help him ensure getting the cast off. I didn't say anything to the contrary because I was enjoying the solitude.

When the tech came to guide him back to have the X-rays done, I flipped through a magazine. Then I went back with him to talk to the doctor because I couldn't trust him to tell me the truth about his care going forward. If I left it up to him, he'd tell me that they said he could resume all activities, including driving. So, in order to avoid an argument, I followed him back to the room with the nurse leading.

Fia came into the examination room after a short wait. She held the X-rays and put them up on the light board to show us. "Good news," she said. "Things are healing up nicely, so I think we can remove the cast today."

"Thank God," GG said.

"Amen to that," I added.

Fia smirked, but stayed professional. "I'm just going to send you over across the hall and Rachel will get that taken care of."

GG got up and left, and Fia said, "How are you?"

"I'm good. Thanks again for having me for dinner. It was really nice."

"Are you kidding? I was so glad you came."

"Hey, I know you're busy, but I have a question I was hoping you might be able to help me answer."

"Happy to try," she said.

After a brief explanation, I said, "Do you know anything about superfecundation in twins?"

"Sure. It's obviously quite rare, but it can happen.

We studied a case in med school."

"So, it's twins that have different fathers?"

"So, in the case of a heteropaternal superfecundation, technically, it's not twins. They would be considered genetic half-siblings, right? It's quite fascinating actually, because if an additional egg is released, it can be fertilized within hours or up to several days, and if that fertilization happens with another person, then biologically, the father of the two developed fetuses is not the same."

I shook my head in disbelief. "Wow."

"Like I said, it's incredibly rare, but can happen, usually when twins are common in the lineage. Do you have other twins in your family?"

"Not that I'm aware of."

"Well, you are going to need to keep me informed," she said.

"I will. Thanks for the information."

"Anytime. In fact, we should have lunch sometime. We didn't get enough time to catch up at dinner."

"I'd love that."

"You still have my number, right?"

"Yep. Your mom wrote it down on a piece of paper for me."

She laughed. "Sounds about right. Please do use it, okay?"

"I will."

****

GG and I got back in the truck and while we were both ready to celebrate his newfound freedom, it hadn't taken very long at the clinic, so it was too early to stop for our usual lunch by the tracks. I hated taking him right back to the farm though, so I offered to stop at the lookout anyway. We sat in the truck waiting to see a train chugging over the high bridge before heading home. I was skeptical that we'd see anything today, the clouds being thick and ominous. But GG insisted we wait.

As we sat watching, GG was in a great mood having been freed of the boat anchor weighing him down, in his words, so he was a bit chattier than usual. I was less optimistic about things.

"So, you like this Brad kid, huh?" he asked.

"Yeah. I do. Except if it turns out that Mickey is my dad, then…"

"Ah. I hadn't even thought of that."

"You hadn't? I thought that was maybe why you didn't like him. If that's not why, what is it you don't like about him then?"

"Mickey? I thought we went over this already."

"Not Mickey. Brad."

"What makes you think I don't like Brad?"

"You aren't very nice to him."

"I'm not? Well, it's not intentional."

I rolled my eyes. "Does it have something to do with the farm? Do you plan to leave it to Max and you're worried it might be Brad's someday if you do?"

"You think I'd leave the farm to Max?"

"I mean…yeah. I assumed. Mom certainly can't take care of it and Max has been the only other person to love it as much as you."

"The Andersen family farm won't go to the Finley's. It will go to you."

"Me?"

"Absolutely," GG said.

"That's…a lot of pressure."

"No pressure. After I'm gone, I don't care what you

do with it, but it will be your decision to make."

"Won't Mom be a little upset by that?"

"We discussed it. She agreed with me that it was the best thing. It's all been written up in my will in the safe."

"Okay. Well, who knows, maybe I'll become a master gardener or something."

GG snorted. "I don't doubt you can do whatever you put your mind to."

"So, then, explain to me why you don't like Brad."

"I was simply reserving my opinion of him, but I saw the way he was looking at you at the wedding. I can see that he cares about you. All I care about is that he treats you right," GG said.

"He does."

And just then, the clouds seemed to part and the sky turned a soft blue as we heard the familiar toot of a train whistle blowing in the distance. "Here she comes!" GG hooted.

We got out of the truck and stood near the edge of the bluff to get a better sightline on the stretch of train as it crossed over the river on the rusty old trestle that perched high over the water. I had watched this exact event take place a million times with my grandfather, but it never got old. Sure, I enjoyed the scene, but mostly it was the joy on GG's face that I couldn't get enough of. He was like a kid on Christmas morning. Today, he threw his arm up and he whooped as the train made its way. We watched it all the way until it was out of sight.

When we got back in the truck, I asked him, "How many times do you think you've seen a train cross that bridge in your life?"

"Oh, probably hundreds."

"But you still love it, don't you?"

"My dad brought me here often when I was a little boy. The lookout wasn't here back then. It was just a regular old bluff, so we'd hike our way down to the water, sometimes we'd have a lunch packed, and fishing poles over our shoulders, and we'd make a whole day of it. It was a simpler time. I have good memories of it, and I just wanted to pass them on to you."

"Really? You've never told me that story before."

"That would sort of defeat the purpose, wouldn't it?"

"Well, you have, you know? Passed the good memories on."

He grunted.

"GG? I don't want you to think that me looking for my dad has anything to do with you. You've been an amazing father-figure to me. It's not about you, you know that right?"

He didn't say anything, so I went on. "It means a lot to me…having your blessing about seeing Brad."

He turned to me. "It means a lot to me, everything you've done for me since Gram died."

"Oh, I didn't do it for you," I teased. "I'm doing it for her. I don't want her haunting me."

He chuckled. "I don't blame you there."

****

That afternoon, after I tended to Grammy's garden, I brought my sketch pad out to the maple tree and sat down under it for shade. I was just planning to doodle, but I couldn't stop thinking about the train trestle. Before I realized it, I'd sketched what could be the beginning of a cute little children's book. I'd been doing commissioned work for a few years, but I'd always wanted to take things a step further and create my own.

Now, I had the freedom to try to accomplish it. And I also had the time. In fact, pouring my thoughts into something else for the next few days would be a great way to deal with the waiting.

I made myself some storyboard grids and I started to fill things in. I worked on it until it was time to go inside and start dinner, but I was fairly pleased with the progress. It being my first foray into children's books though, I knew the next step would be to actually show it to someone for feedback. That was the part that terrified me. I was definitely not ready to show it to GG, so I needed to find someone else. I thought I had a pretty good idea who that someone might be.

Chapter Thirty-Three

After dinner, while GG was reading his paper, I drove over to the bar. It was relatively quiet. I stayed far away from the "Uncle Mickey" beverage formally known as a Hart's now that I knew it triggered my panic. I also had the bottle of peppermint oil in my purse just in case an attack should rear itself unexpectedly.

I'd also been thinking a lot about what Brad said about how he'd gotten to rely too heavily on alcohol to avoid dealing with his issues and I could see where I'd been doing that a little too much myself since being back, so I ordered a sparkling water.

"What do you think?" he said when he returned with it. "Knowing that this place could be part yours someday?" He flashed a smile and swung his arms around like a model on a gameshow.

"I…"

"And when I say that, I'm hoping it's by legal arrangement instead of genetics," he added.

"Oh? Is this a proposal?" I teased.

"I mean…who could say no to this prize?" He waved his arms around again.

I laughed. "Well, depending on how things go, I'm getting a pretty good picture of my future today."

"Huh?"

"GG told me earlier that he's leaving me the farm. So, if things go right for you, you might end up learning to milk the cows after all."

"Oh no! I've spent my whole life trying to avoid that exact thing."

"Yeah. But fate might have other plans for you."

"Well, I've heard of worse fates. Besides, as much as I joke about it, I actually do have a soft spot for the farm."

"Yeah? Me too."

"I can just imagine Gus rolling over in his grave watching the two of us trying to manage his farm after he dies."

I laughed. "He won't be in a grave. The family all rests in the apple orchard. I learned that recently."

"Really? That's…kind of nice, actually."

"It is."

Brad went off to help a few more patrons who came in, so I pulled my sketch book and pencil out of my bag and I continued to add some more details to my mock-up of the train book.

When Brad came back, he said, "What are you up to?"

"I came up with an idea today for a children's book."

"Oh, yeah? Can I see?"

"Okay, but I just started it and it's still pretty rough." I was about to slide it toward him when I pulled it back. "And, the sketches are really just outlined at this point. There's no color yet or anything."

He nodded, but I stayed hunched over the paper, unsure if I was really ready to unveil it. Brad just looked at me, waiting patiently as I cycled through the entire artist quandary. Was it good enough? What if he hated it? Did I want to put him in that awkward position of trying to fake it, or worse yet, what if he couldn't fake it?

"On second thought, I'm not sure if I should show you yet. It's not ready."

"Come on…I'm sure it's amazing."

"Thanks, but I just realized it still needs more work. Can I show you in a few days?"

"Sure."

"Sorry."

"Don't be," he said.

I put the sketch pad safely away back in my bag and said, "Oh, I was going to ask you…do you want to come to the brunch at Mom and Ernie's place with me on Sunday?"

"Are you asking me on a date?"

"God, no. This is more like a family obligation."

"I thought you wanted to talk to your mom after?"

"I do. You don't have to stay for that part…unless you want to stay for that part?"

Brad laughed. "I think you'll have better luck without me there."

"Hmm…I'm not so sure about that, but yeah. You're probably right. I should do it on my own."

"How did the doctor appointment go? Did Gus get his cast removed?"

"He did! And he's so much more agreeable now."

"I can only imagine."

"Guess what else," I told him, pulling my phone out. "I found this and I asked Fia about it at the appointment." I tilted the screen to show him the picture I took with the definition. "I had never even heard of it before, but she confirmed that it's real. It's rare, but it can happen."

"Jesus. You think this is what happened?"

"I have no idea, but so far it makes the most sense of anything else we've come up with."

"Just when I start to think we've seen it all, your mom somehow manages to throw another match on the flame."

"That is pretty much her thing."

"So, if it's true, it could be that Mickey is Sonny's dad, and you have a totally different dad, but you were born on the same day."

"Yup. Fia said it would technically make us half-siblings, not even twins."

"That's nuts."

"I know."

Brad went to help another customer and I had another burst of creative energy pop into my head, so I opened my sketch pad back up and continued to draw, roughing out a few more scenes of the book. When he came back, I closed the cover.

"You are serious about not letting me see, huh?"

"I will. Just not yet."

He playfully tried to grab it out of my grip. "Come on, Lu…"

I released it. "Did you just call me Lu? You've never called me that before."

"Sorry. I didn't mean to…it just came out."

"No. It's good. I like it."

"Yeah? Okay. Lu it is then."

I nodded.

"Now can I see your illustrations?"

"No." I pulled the pad back. "But I appreciate that you called them illustrations."

"Huh?"

"Oh, nothing. It's just that when I went to Fia's for dinner last weekend, one of her husband's friends referred to what I do as coloring pictures for a living."

"What a jerk. It wasn't my middle-school nemesis Arthur Morton, was it?"

"The guy who started the rumor about your mom? No. This guy's name was Johan."

"Johan? I don't know him, but if I did, I would kick his ass for you."

"You'd do that for me?"

"Absolutely."

"Was it a date?"

"I never asked, but it did feel a bit like it was meant as a set up."

"Yeah. I'm definitely going to kick his ass then."

As the night progressed, more people started to trickle in, but Brad continued to come and fill my water glass. He even brought me a basket of hot French fries. We flirted innocently when he had a moment to spare and when he didn't I continued to sketch. Lost in the drawing, I didn't even notice that the guy sitting next to me was the same guy who'd been talking to Kelsey when I was here a while back. He was no longer wearing a brown pleather jacket because it was the height of summer, but I recognized him all the same. He must have recognized me as well because he leaned over to me and said, "You're the out of town girl, aren't you?"

"Oh, yep. That's me."

"I recognize you now. You're Gus and Ida's grandkid, aren't you?"

I smiled at him. "I am."

"I'm really good with faces, so it had been bugging me since that night I saw you last. That makes you Jenny Andersen's daughter, then, right?"

"It does."

"I'm Jake Bower. I own Bower Auto Shop on the

corner of Arrow and Amber."

"Nice to meet you, Jake."

"Oh, we've met before. I remember when your granddad used to bring you by in his old Ford. You were just a tiny thing back then though."

"She's still running. The Ford," I said. "I drove it here."

"That right? Doesn't surprise me. Gus babied that truck."

"He sure did."

"Well, I haven't seen Brad this happy in a long time. You two got something going?"

"Us? No."

"What? Come on…you're pulling my leg."

"I'm not."

"What's the problem then?"

"The problem is that we might be cousins, Jake." I blushed just saying that out loud to a virtual stranger in a bar.

"You're shitting me?"

"I wish I were."

He thought about it. "Mickey's daughter?"

"Possibly."

He looked at me again with an intense gaze. "No. I don't see it."

I shrugged.

"Well, ain't that the rub."

"It really is."

"Doesn't your mom know who fathered you?"

"If she does, she hasn't told me."

"Have you done the DNA thing?"

"Not yet."

"Well, you gotta."

"Yes. I guess we do."

"I hope it works out," Jake said.

"Thanks."

The next time Brad came back around, I told him I needed to head out.

"I'll walk you out. Alton's a dangerous place at night."

"Very scary out there," I said.

The night air was fresh compared to that circulating inside the bar. It was clear and there it was, like it was following me around. Another half-moon lit up the usually dark parking lot. I took a deep breath, feeling somewhat settled for no reason at all.

When we reached the truck, Brad said, "I saw Jake flapping his jaw at you. What was that all about?"

"Oh, he was fine."

"Good. He's not a bad guy, just a little overly nosey sometimes."

"I kinda like him. I'm starting to feel like a regular myself."

"Yeah. Keep it up and people will start creating their own rumors about you."

"Oh, I think Jake might have a few thoughts on the two of us."

"That's what I was afraid of," he said.

"It's a hazard of this place. Wouldn't happen in the Big Apple," I teased. "Okay. So, I'll see you at brunch on Sunday, right?"

"Sure."

"Oh, and I almost forgot, Ernie's taking all of the men golfing after, so if you're up for that, that's a thing that's happening."

"Golfing, eh?"

"Apparently. Do you play golf at all?"

"I mean…I've golfed a time or two."

"You don't have to go, if you don't want to."

"Yeah. No. It could be fun."

"Okay, then plan for that."

"I will."

"Goodnight, Brad Finley."

"Night, Lu."

Chapter Thirty-Four

Sunday finally managed to come around and not a moment too soon. I was so ready to have this whole thing over with, I almost actually wanted to go to the party. GG, on the other hand, opted out. Max was around and so was another young farmhand he was starting to show the ropes to, so I decided to let GG stay behind. He would not have enjoyed watching Mom and Ernie open wedding gifts. I don't know who enjoyed that, except the people receiving the gifts, but whatever.

I picked Brad up and almost died laughing when I saw what he was wearing. He'd clearly gone shopping for a new golf outfit because he came out in checkered, lemon-yellow shorts with a white polo shirt.

"New outfit?" I asked.

"The guy at the sports store told me this was what people wear on the course."

"Admit it. You've never been golfing before."

"Is it that obvious?"

"You could have just said no."

"What? No. This will be a good opportunity for me to get to know Ernie a little bit better."

"Oh, I see. You're trying to get on his good side early, eh?"

"I would like to be on the good side of one of your family members," he said.

"That's cute."

On the drive over, Brad said, "Are you nervous about talking to your mom?"

"How'd you guess?"

"Because you've been biting your fingernails the entire drive."

I pulled my finger out of my mouth. "Sorry."

He put his hand on my knee. "Just remember to breathe."

I looked down at his hand and he quickly pulled it back.

"Just remember that when you talk to your mom, picture me on the golf course making a complete ass out of myself."

"I don't even need to do that. I just need to think of you in this outfit."

"Is it that bad?"

"Yes. Sorry."

"Well, anything to help you through this whole thing," he said.

"I appreciate it."

When we pulled up, I was feeling a bit better about things. There were a few cars already in the driveway, which was good because I didn't want to be the first to arrive. I didn't actually want to be alone with my mother until it was completely necessary.

Inside, the atmosphere was light and cheery. A spread of food was set out on the table. The home, though it had a ski chalet feel on the outside, was actually airy and minimalist inside. The living room had a stone fireplace with a skylight window above it that filled in the A of the frame and let in tons of light.

Brad and I said hello to my mom and Ernie. "Grab a plate of food and a drink and take it out back," Ernie said to us. We did as instructed and went out a sliding glass patio door to a massive deck that looked out and down into a ravine with a stream running through it.

"Wow. This is some backyard," Brad said.

"It's beautiful."

We sat down on folding chairs set up surrounding the pile of gifts. I had hemmed and hawed on what to get them, but when I was back in New York I'd picked up a blown glass vase from one of the many artist lofts in my old neighborhood. I realized now it would go nicely with their current décor, though I was still nervous to have my mother open it in front of a crowd of strangers. I had no idea what she'd say about it.

A man sitting next to me introduced himself as Tommy, one of Ernie's buddies from the fire department. "Oh, I remember you. You were there that day when my grandpa had his accident."

"I was. How's old Gus doing?"

"He's all healed up now and as feisty as ever."

"That's what we like to hear."

We chatted for a bit longer and ate our food, and then Mom and Ernie came out and sat down. Ernie thanked everyone for coming. They told a quick story about their honeymoon and then they started opening the gifts. It seemed to drone on and on. The pile of boxes and envelopes seemed to be diminishing at a snail's pace, and after a while some people got up to stretch. Tommy turned to me and asked if I minded if he smoked. I said it was fine.

He lit up and after the second puff, I started to feel a little off. I turned to Brad and asked if he wanted to take a walk down to the stream. I thought maybe the fresh air would help. He nodded and we got up to go, but as much as I tried to pull it back, I was sliding. I didn't want it to happen here in front of all of these people, but before I could stop it, I went down. I heard a few people yelp and my mother hollered my name.

The next thing I knew, the strong scent of peppermint was inside of my nostrils and I was coming out of it. I blinked a few times. I was cradled in Brad's lap. I saw a full circle of faces surrounding me, staring down at me in alarm. Ernie was at my side, checking my pulse. I tried to sit up.

"Hey," Ernie said. "Take it easy. Don't get up too quickly."

"What's going on?" my mother asked. "What happened to her?"

"She had a panic attack," Brad said.

"Why?" she asked.

"I don't know," he said, "but I think she's coming out of it now."

"What did you just give her? What is that?"

"It's peppermint oil."

"Peppermint oil? Why?"

"Mickey gave it to us," he said.

With a straight view to my mother's face, I saw every muscle in it twitch upon hearing his name. Brad, immediately realizing what he'd said, looked at me.

"I'm okay," I said. "I can get up now. You guys go on with the party. Brad and I will just get some fresh air."

"Are you sure that's a good idea?" my mother asked.

"It's okay," Ernie said. "Her vitals are stable."

She nodded and Brad helped me up.

We walked off the deck and down to the ravine. We sat down near the stream and I took my sandals off so I could dip my feet. "God, that was so embarrassing. I've never had it happen like that before in the middle of a large group of people."

"I thought maybe you were faking it so we could get out of there," Brad teased.

"It wouldn't have been the worst idea."

We both laughed.

"You sure you're okay?"

"Yeah. Thanks. I should have thought of the peppermint oil, but I thought once I was away from there, I'd be okay."

"What caused it? Do you have any idea?"

"I think it was the cigarette smoke. Just like at Mickey's. Clearly another trigger. I just haven't been around smoke much since it's not legal indoors anymore."

"That makes sense," he said. "I'm sorry about blurting that out about Mickey. I didn't think."

"It's okay. It's gonna come out soon anyway. At least I hope it is."

"Maybe I should stay here with you, in case it happens again."

"You trying to get out of golfing?"

"No. Honestly. I'm just worried about leaving you," he said.

"I'll be okay. I'll keep the peppermint in my hands this time."

"Okay. Should we head back?"

"Let's wait a little while longer. I want to make sure my mom finishes opening the presents before we return. I was dreading having her open my gift in front of people."

"Why?"

"I don't know. It's just a vase. I think maybe it's a

little cold and impersonal for a wedding gift for my mother and knowing her, she'll have something to say about it."

"I gotcha."

By the time we got back, the gifts had all been opened and many of the guests had started to trickle out. The men who were going golfing were making their way to the front of the house to start loading up their gear. Brad was going to rent a set of clubs at the course, so he didn't have any gear to load, but he was riding with Ernie, so he went out with them to wait.

"I'll call you later," I told him.

"Okay."

"Have fun. Remember you're trying to get the lowest score."

"Right." He smiled and headed out.

In the kitchen, I helped put the food away while my mom said goodbye to the last few guests. After everyone had gone, my mom sat on the sofa in the living room with a stack of crinkled gift wrapping in front of her on the coffee table. I went in to join her, sitting in the arm chair across from her.

Her eyes remained on the perfect creases she made into a piece of paper, but she said, "Feeling better?"

"Yeah."

"Is there something going on with you and Bradley?"

I shook my head, adamantly. "No."

"I see how you two look at each other."

"Would it be bad if there was something between us?" I asked.

"That's your business," she said.

"Mom…I saw Mickey Finley."

251

She nodded, but continued to fold.

"I know he was there that night, the night Sonny… Anyway, he told me that Sonny was his daughter. Is that true?"

She sighed and looked at me. "You and Bradley are not cousins if that's what you're asking me."

"That's not what I'm asking you!"

"What is it then?"

"Why was Mickey there? Why does he think Sonny was his? I want the truth this time!"

I saw my mother's hands trembling a bit as she took a new piece of wrapping paper and pressed it on her leg to smooth it out.

"Mom, I'm serious. I'm going to take a DNA test. Please, just tell me what happened."

"Mickey and I were in love at one time. Yes."

"And?"

"Then I started to see what your grandparents had warned me against. They were right. I was wrong. I thought it would all be over when I went off to college, but Mickey had different thoughts. He kept coming around. His drinking got worse. He started hanging out with other bikers he'd met in the city." She paused, took another piece of paper and fiddled with it in her hands. "He…started to hit me."

"God."

"I didn't know what to do. I no longer loved him, and worse than that, I was scared of him. I felt foolish to have been caught up in things with him. I was just hoping he'd eventually leave me alone. Then I met another man. He was an art student in my program. He wasn't anything like Michael. He was kind and gentle. Things started to finally go well for me for the first time…and then I found out that I was pregnant."

She took a deep breath and folded the paper she had crinkled in her hands. "When I had you, I could see immediately that Sonny had Michael's features and you didn't. I asked the doctor if it could be possible…and he ran some tests and determined it was." A tear trickled down her cheek. She quickly wiped it away.

"So, I was right? We aren't twins, are we?"

She shook her head. "It was funny because I named you and you both held true to those names. Your sister was mischievous and rebellious and you were my sweet, quiet girl. You were nothing alike. You were night and day. Sort of like your fathers."

"Michael knew about the pregnancy but nothing more. When you were born, he insisted on seeing his child, so I kept you from him, and I let him see Sonny occasionally. I never left her alone with him, mind you. Anyway, I hadn't seen or heard anything from him in a long time. I thought it was over. I wasn't expecting him that night. He showed up drunker than a skunk. He was shouting. I told him to go home, but he tried to bust my door down. It was late. The neighbors were getting upset."

"So, Mickey was the one trying to break in?"

She nodded. "I thought that if I just let him in for a minute, if he saw Sonny, he'd leave. I was trying to defuse the situation. I opened the door and brought your sister out into the living room. I thought after he saw her, he'd leave, but he wanted to take Sonny with him. He grabbed her out of my arms. I tried pulling her back. She was screaming and he wouldn't let go. That's when Jeffrey came out of the bedroom and the two of them argued. Michael had a gun. It all happened so fast. I tried to get Sonny out of there, but…"

"Wait. The gun was Mickey's?"

"Yes. He'd gotten mixed up in some kind of biker gang. I don't know. Like I said, I wanted nothing to do with him at that point, but I was stuck."

"But…Jeffrey was the one who shot Sonny?"

She nodded. "He didn't mean to do it. It was an accident. Like I said, it all happened so fast. He saw that Michael was trying to take Sonny. He didn't know who Michael was. They fought. Michael dropped the gun in the tussle and Jeffrey was only trying to grab it away from him, but it went off. And Sonny was in the middle of them when it did." She took a big breath. "He was trying to protect us."

"But they arrested him?"

"We were young. The cops didn't believe a word of it. And Jeffrey had long hair at the time too. He wasn't a biker. He was a hippy. Still, the police assumed it was some kind of drug related thing or something. I don't know." She sniffled. "I tried to convince Jeffrey to let Michael take the fall, but he was too good. He wouldn't do it. And I had to give custody of you over to your grandparents or else you would have been taken away…gone to foster care."

"What? That's why you signed away your parental rights?"

"Yes. I had no choice. It was the best option."

All this time. I had no idea. "I wish you would have told me."

"How could I? I was so ashamed. I couldn't even look you in the eye."

"So, the reason Mickey didn't know about me was because I wasn't his?"

She nodded again.

"Because my father is Jeffrey Donovan? The man who shot my sister?"

She pulled a tissue from her pocket and dabbed her eyes. "I'm sorry. Now you can see why I couldn't tell you."

Now I was crying too as I tried to process it all.

"I made terrible mistakes," my mother said between the tears. "But I never meant for any of that to happen. I was a young, naïve woman at the time and I was still dealing with my own trauma from losing Robbie. I knew how hard it was going to be for you…to have to go through life without your other half. That's why I couldn't be around much. The farm, and seeing you, it was too much for me…I felt the guilt all over again."

"Wait…Robbie…your other half? Was he…your twin brother?"

"Yes."

"I didn't know that."

"I should have been there…to protect him that day, but we'd had an argument. I wanted to go in the hayloft and doodle the day away in my notepad. He was tired of that. He wanted to do something fun, exciting. We were similar, but different in many ways…like you and Sonny. You won't believe this, but you and I are more alike. I was the shy responsible one, the one who liked to be alone with my art. Had I been with Robbie that day, like I often was, it would never have happened. I would have stopped him."

"Oh, Mom. I'm sorry. That must have been awful."

"I thought I could do better with you. I thought I could protect you, but instead, I failed. I-I promised Jeffrey I wouldn't tell you about him. He was so ashamed. He didn't want you to know what he'd done. He felt such remorse. I felt worse. It was all my fault, really, the whole thing. He was a good man. He was a good dad. He loved you, and he loved Sonny too. Naturally, the whole thing changed him. We couldn't come back from what happened, not together, barely alone. The least I could do was hold up my end of the deal and leave him to live the rest of his life in peace. And I thought not telling you was the best thing for you too. How could a girl understand such a thing? I-I'm sorry, Luna." Her tears flowed freely now. I got up and sat down next to her.

"I'm sorry too." I leaned over and I hugged her. She hugged me back. It was the first time in our lives that we'd been able to do that. When we broke apart, I said, "Can I ask you one more thing? If you knew all along that Mickey wasn't my dad, why do you not want me to be with Brad?"

"I never said I didn't want you to be with him."

"But…it's obvious you don't like him. I see how you look at him."

"It's not that." She sighed again. "It's…well, when I look at him, I see so much of Sonny in him. I see…what she might have grown to be. Bradley is a sweet kid. I just…it pains me sometimes to look at him."

"Oh. I…" I was too stunned to say anything more.

"And, I'll admit, it's a little weird thinking of you with someone who was related to your sister, but…there's nothing wrong with it. You two share no blood. Besides, I saw how he took care of you today. I…want you to be happy, so…you have my blessing."

"Really?"

She nodded. "Yes. Really. If I can't make things

right, it's the least I can do."

"Mom…you don't have to make things right. I…forgive you."

She nodded and we hugged again.

Chapter Thirty-Five

I sat on the beach as the sun went down. While I waited for Brad to arrive, I thought through everything that my mom had told me. It was still sinking in that my father had been living in the same city as me, and also that he had been the one to take Sonny's life. I had less anger about it now, knowing the truth. It hadn't really been his fault. All of my pent-up frustration and rage finally released. And while my mom had a part in all of it, I realized I'd been too hard on her all this time.

So many emotions flowed through me. It was a lot to take in, everything I'd learned in such a short amount of time.

"Hey," Brad said, sitting down in the sand next to me. He was still in his golfing outfit.

"How was the big golf game?"

"Well, I'm tired, sore, sunburnt, and humbled...so, overall, I think it went well. How about you? How'd it go with your mom?"

"It was a lot."

I explained to him what I'd learned. Saying it all out loud made me start to cry again as much as I was trying to hold it together. And I felt bad telling Brad his blood relative had been the catalyst to the death of my sister who was also his cousin.

"I'm so sorry," he said after I finished talking.

"It's crazy. I don't even know how to think about it

all. I just feel…bad."

"Me too. I feel terrible that one of my family members was partially to blame in the whole thing."

"Oh, and my mom told me she doesn't hate you. She said it hurts to look at you because she sees my sister in you."

"That makes me feel bad too."

We sat silently for a long time.

"I totally understand if you can't look at me the same way anymore either," he finally said.

"It's not your fault," I said.

"No, but it's gonna be weird for you too, isn't it? Knowing your twin sister and I were related? That my uncle was violent toward your mother? That…"

"You are nothing like Mickey," I said.

"I…"

Before he could get another word out, I grabbed him by the collar of his golf shirt, pulled him toward me, and I kissed him with all I had. It felt even more intense than when we were teenagers, except that this time, I wasn't experiencing a panic attack. I was experiencing something much, much better than that and I didn't want it to end, but we eventually broke apart. I said, "Nope. Not weird for me. How about you?"

"No," he said, catching his breath. "Not weird at all."

"You know what else? I think we can safely say that the curse is officially broken."

He grinned. "About damn time."

"And it turns out I'm not allergic to you."

"Huh?"

"No panic attack. It proves you aren't a trigger."

"Well, if I was, you'd need a lot more than just that

little bottle of peppermint oil to repel me," he said, leaning in for another kiss.

Afterward, we sat holding hands in the sand like teenagers as the sun set and he said, "What are you going to do now? Are you going to contact Jeffrey?"

"I'm not sure yet."

"What about Mickey? Are you going to call him?"

"No. I don't think so."

"If you want me to kick his ass, I will."

I laughed and put my head on his shoulder. As we sat there together on the beach, the sun faded away and the moon became visible. Tonight, it was no longer a half circle, but a full, complete circle.

****

A few days later, Brad asked me to go on a real first date with him, which I happily accepted. He wouldn't tell me anything about it except that I should bring along my art supplies. I laughed at that and asked for more specifics. After some back and forth, I figured out that he meant my sketch pad and pencil.

I was surprised when we ended up in Marina at an actual boat marina, where he'd rented a pontoon for us. He had a picnic dinner in a cooler that he'd brought along and loaded it onto the boat along with some other gear, and then we set sail.

"This is really amazing," I told him as we cruised along the river. "Thank you."

"Well, I know how much you love sitting by the water, so I thought you might also enjoy sitting on top of it."

"I do. It's crazy how little I've actually been on a boat considering how close the river was to me growing up. How'd you learn to drive a boat?"

"Well, that's where I'm ahead of you because while I might not be a golfer, I can fish."

"Really? Another interesting fact about you that I did not know."

Brad captained the boat over to a perfect spot practically under the train trestle before he stopped the boat and threw out the anchor.

"I thought it would help inspire you," he said.

"This is perfect. And I don't just mean the location."

He smiled and baited his hook, while I pulled out my sketch pad and did some drawing for my book. After an hour or so, we ate the food Brad made and then I finally showed him the pages I'd been working on intently for the last several days.

"Wow. I had no idea you could draw like this. The story is great too."

"You think so?"

"I do. Have you shown it to your grandpa yet?"

"No. I'm terrified."

He laughed. "I think he'll love it. I love it."

"Thanks." I bit my lip and said, "Can I ask you something? Do you…want kids at all someday maybe?"

"Me? Honestly, it's funny because I'd never given it much thought. I'd always assumed I'd never get married or anything like that, but…recently, I've been thinking about it some. I'll admit."

"Oh? So…is that a yes?"

"Uh huh. What about you?"

"Well, it's the same for me then."

"Okay, then," he said.

"Although, I should warn you…twins run in my family. Do you want to change your answer?"

He laughed. "I mean…as long as the twins both

belonged to me, then I'd be okay with that."

"I don't think that should be a problem."

"All right. Twins it is," he said.

It was a perfect first date, but it had to end because I was still worried about leaving GG alone for too long. Brad understood and he came back to the farm with me. After GG went to sleep that night we hiked up to the hill, spread out some sleeping bags, and we finished what we'd started all those years ago, though not a ton of sleeping took place.

In the morning, we went back to the house before GG woke up. I told Brad he didn't have to leave, but he was adamant about trying to stay on my grandpa's good side, or at least not on his bad side. I kissed him on the porch and watched him drive off.

Chapter Thirty-Six

The summer months rushed by as they were famous for doing in the Midwest, and a strong autumn breeze blew across the prairie. I'd made another big life decision and it was time to let everyone know, so I'd invited the whole family for dinner. I'd already told Brad because I couldn't keep it from him, but I was still nervous about telling the rest of the family. The fact that I had a family to invite to dinner was still a concept I'd only just begun to grasp.

I was digging in the dirt in Grammy's garden harvesting some of the vegetables I'd managed to grow which also felt like a miracle. I'd had lots of help from GG and Max, but I was proud of what I'd accomplished. I think Grammy would have been too. I probably looked ridiculous. I was wearing her old straw hat and garden gloves. As I plucked a carrot and shook the dirt off of it to place it into my basket, I saw Brad coming toward me. "Never thought I'd have the hots for a farmer," he said, stopping and leaning against the little garden fencing.

"Well, it turns out that growing food is very therapeutic," I told him. "At least that's what the therapist told me in my session with her earlier today."

"Yeah? How'd it go?"

"It was good, I think."

"She's not terrible, right?"

"No. She's been helping me work through things a

lot actually," I said.

"That's great." He paused and gave me a sad smile. "So…you're leaving again."

"You know why I have to go."

"I do. I'll miss you though."

"Come on," I said, taking off my garden gloves. "We have to finish dinner before Mom and Ernie get here."

We went inside and Brad helped me wash and cut up the veggies for the salad.

GG stood at the stove stirring the apple cider sauce we'd begun simmering earlier in the day from tomatoes from the garden and apples from Sonny and Grammy's tree. I couldn't get over the fact that most of the ingredients of the meal had been grown right here on the Andersen farm. Even Brad was impressed by this, though I could tell he was growing weary of hearing me brag about it.

When Mom and Ernie came in, I started the pasta and Mom helped set the table. I realized that it would be the first time in a very long time when all five of the chairs at the old oak table would be in use. It felt like we were a real family having a normal dinner together. If only I wasn't nervous about what I had to say.

As we sat down to eat, my jitters reared up again so I decided it was time to get it over with. I made my announcement to the family.

"So, as you guys know, Brad and I took DNA tests, just to be sure…And, well, we got the results. It turns out…"

"For goodness sake, Luna. Please, just tell us," my mother said.

"I'm not kissing my cousin," Brad blurted out.

"Good," GG muttered.

My mother nodded, but I could see that she was also relieved and her shoulders relaxed.

"But, there's more." I paused because this was the hard part. "I've been emailing Jeffrey—my dad—these last few weeks. While I've been making good progress with the nightmares and the panic attacks as it is, my therapist said she thinks the next step is for me to meet him in person. And Jeffrey seems eager and willing to do that, so I'm headed back to New York...I'm leaving tomorrow."

I stopped and looked at my mother. Her tense shoulders had returned a bit, so I went on. "Mom? Are you okay with it? Because if you aren't, I could rethink it, or—"

She looked at me and smiled. "No. You should go."

"Really?"

"Yes. Obviously, the therapist knows best, so I want you to do what you need to do."

"I'll only be gone for a week and Brad is going to stay here with GG, but if you wouldn't mind popping in on the nights when he's working..."

"I'll be fine," GG interjected.

"We will," my mother said.

"Thanks." I cleared my throat. "The other reason I'm going is because I have a few meetings lined up. I've pitched my children's book to a few friends I have who work in publishing and they'd like to see it. And, I figured, since I'd be there, I'd like to show them in person since the proof looks better that way."

"That's really wonderful," my mother said. "I'd love to see it too."

"You would?"

"Absolutely."

"I…can show you after dinner."

"What's it about?" Ernie asked.

"Well, it's about a boy who runs away after a tragedy in his family and he sets off trying to get to his grandfather's house, but he loses his way. And he realizes he has to stop and ask for help because he has to cross the high bridge. I'm tentatively calling it *Over the River*."

"I like it," my mother said.

"Me too," GG said, giving me a wink.

Relieved to have that over with, I dug into my food. Everyone else followed my lead.

"The food is fantastic," Ernie said.

"It was a group effort," I said, thinking of Sonny and Grammy and all of the family members who came before us. I imagined them around the table with us filling in the empty space. I couldn't believe how content I felt.

After we finished eating and after Brad helped me with the dishes, I served dessert, and I passed the book around for everyone to see. They were all complimentary, including my mother. Her comments were sincere and that made me feel more confident about pitching it.

After Mom and Ernie left, Brad and I went out onto the porch and sat on the swing. He held my hand. "You promise you'll be back this time, right?" he teased.

"I promise. And a week should feel like nothing compared to a decade."

"I dunno. I'm still gonna miss you."

"I'm going to miss you too." I kissed him softly. "Thank you for staying. I know it's a little weird for you."

"I can handle it. If you can meet your dad, I can hang out with Gus for a few days."

I nodded. "He has promised to be on his best behavior."

"His best behavior is still a little scary."

I laughed. "True. And you'll tend to my garden for me, right?"

"I can't guarantee anything will still be alive when you get back, but I'll try."

"Lucky for you, the season is almost over."

"Yeah. I was also secretly planning to have my dad do it, so…"

I smacked his leg. "You better not!"

"Okay. Fine. I'll do it. I can't believe you've turned into a farmer on me. This was never part of the deal."

"Somebody is going to have to run this place someday," I teased.

"I'll handle the books."

"That is a deal," I said.

"Are you sure you're going to be okay? You've got your peppermint oil packed, right?"

"I even bought a backup at the pharmacy the other day, just in case," I said.

"Good. Call me as soon as the meeting is over."

"Which one? The one with my dad or the publisher? Because I'm not sure which one I'm more scared about," I said.

"Oh. Right. Both!"

"I will." I put my head down on his shoulder and looked up at the stars beginning to pop as I reflected on the last few months. So much had happened that I felt like a totally different person. I was no longer the same broken woman who had stepped off that plane dreading every moment of being back in Alton. This time I knew that I would count down the minutes until I returned. This place finally felt like home to me after almost thirty years. I was happy, in love, and moving toward feeling more and more like a whole person.

A word about the author...

Jody is a life-long Twin Citian, a wife, and mother. She got the writing bug while reporting for her high school newspaper, and received a degree in Communications from the University of Minnesota. While starting a family, she began writing fiction and has since been published in The Keepthings and Mystery Magazine Weekly.